JULIAN BARNES

The Sense of an Ending

VINTAGE

1 3 5 7 9 10 8 6 4 2

Vintage
20 Vauxhall Bridge Road,
London SW1V 2SA

Vintage is part of the Penguin Random House
group of companies whose addresses can be found at
global.penguinrandomhouse.com

Penguin
Random House
UK

This edition published in Vintage in 2017
First published in Vintage in 2012
First published in hardback by Jonathan Cape in 2011

penguin.co.uk/vintage

A CIP catalogue record for this book is available
from the British Library

ISBN 9781784707989

Printed and bound by Clays Ltd, St Ives plc

Penguin Random House is committed to a sustainable future
for our business, our readers and our planet. This book is made
from Forest Stewardship Council® certified paper.

MIX
Paper from
responsible sources
FSC® C018179

for Pat

ONE

I remember, in no particular order:

– a shiny inner wrist;

– steam rising from a wet sink as a hot frying pan is laughingly tossed into it;

– gouts of sperm circling a plughole, before being sluiced down the full length of a tall house;

– a river rushing nonsensically upstream, its wave and wash lit by half a dozen chasing torchbeams;

– another river, broad and grey, the direction of its flow disguised by a stiff wind exciting the surface;

– bathwater long gone cold behind a locked door.

This last isn't something I actually saw, but what you end up remembering isn't always the same as what you have witnessed.

We live in time – it holds us and moulds us – but I've never felt I understood it very well. And I'm not referring to theories about how it bends and doubles back, or may exist elsewhere in parallel versions. No, I mean ordinary, everyday time, which clocks and watches assure us passes regularly: tick-tock, click-clock. Is there anything more plausible than a second hand? And yet it takes only the smallest pleasure or pain to teach us time's malleability. Some emotions speed it up, others slow it down; occasionally, it seems to go missing – until the eventual point when it really does go missing, never to return.

I'm not very interested in my schooldays, and don't feel any nostalgia for them. But school is where it all began, so I need to return briefly to a few incidents that have grown into anecdotes, to some approximate memories which time has deformed into certainty. If I can't be sure of the actual events any more, I can at least be true to the impressions those facts left. That's the best I can manage.

There were three of us, and he now made the fourth. We hadn't expected to add to our tight number: cliques and pairings had happened long before, and we were already beginning to imagine our escape from school into life. His name was Adrian Finn, a tall, shy boy who initially kept his eyes down and his mind to himself. For the first day or two, we took little notice of him: at our school there was no welcoming ceremony, let alone its opposite, the punitive induction. We just registered his presence and waited.

The masters were more interested in him than we were. They had to work out his intelligence and sense of discipline, calculate how well he'd previously been taught, and if he might prove 'scholarship material'. On the third morning of that autumn term, we had a history class with Old Joe Hunt, wryly affable in his three-piece suit, a teacher whose system of control depended on maintaining sufficient but not excessive boredom.

'Now, you'll remember that I asked you to do some preliminary reading about the reign of Henry VIII.' Colin, Alex and I squinted at one another, hoping that the question wouldn't be flicked, like an angler's fly, to land on one of our heads. 'Who might like to offer a characterisation of the age?' He drew his own conclusion from our averted eyes. 'Well, Marshall, perhaps. How would you describe Henry VIII's reign?'

Our relief was greater than our curiosity, because Marshall was a cautious know-nothing who lacked the inventiveness of true ignorance. He searched for possible hidden complexities in the question before eventually locating a response.

'There was unrest, sir.'

An outbreak of barely controlled smirking; Hunt himself almost smiled.

'Would you, perhaps, care to elaborate?'

Marshall nodded slow assent, thought a little longer, and decided it was no time for caution. 'I'd say there was great unrest, sir.'

'Finn, then. Are you up in this period?'

The new boy was sitting a row ahead and to my left. He had shown no evident reaction to Marshall's idiocies.

'Not really, sir, I'm afraid. But there is one line of thought according to which all you can truly say of any historical event – even the outbreak of the First World War, for example – is that "something happened".'

'Is there, indeed? Well, that would put me out of a job, wouldn't it?' After some sycophantic laughter, Old Joe Hunt pardoned our holiday idleness and filled us in on the polygamous royal butcher.

At the next break, I sought out Finn. 'I'm Tony Webster.' He looked at me warily. 'Great line to Hunt.' He seemed not to know what I was referring to. 'About something happening.'

'Oh. Yes. I was rather disappointed he didn't take it up.'

That wasn't what he was supposed to say.

Another detail I remember: the three of us, as a symbol of our bond, used to wear our watches with the face on the inside of the wrist. It was an affectation, of course, but perhaps something more. It made time feel like a personal, even a secret, thing. We expected Adrian to note the gesture, and follow suit; but he didn't.

Later that day – or perhaps another day – we had a double English period with Phil Dixon, a young master just down from Cambridge. He liked to use contemporary texts, and would throw out sudden challenges. '"Birth, and Copulation, and Death" – that's what T. S. Eliot says it's all about. Any comments?' He once compared a Shakespearean hero to Kirk Douglas in *Spartacus*. And I remember how, when we were discussing Ted Hughes's poetry, he put his head at a donnish slant and murmured, 'Of course, we're all wondering what will happen when he runs out of animals.' Sometimes, he addressed us as 'Gentlemen'. Naturally, we adored him.

That afternoon, he handed out a poem with no title, date or author's name, gave us ten minutes to study it, then asked for our responses.

'Shall we start with you, Finn? Put simply, what would you say this poem is *about*?'

Adrian looked up from his desk. 'Eros and Thanatos, sir.'

'Hmm. Go on.'

'Sex and death,' Finn continued, as if it might not just be the thickies in the back row who didn't understand Greek. 'Or love and death, if you prefer. The erotic principle, in any case, coming into conflict with the death principle. And what ensues from that conflict. Sir.'

I was probably looking more impressed than Dixon thought healthy.

'Webster, enlighten us further.'

'I just thought it was a poem about a barn owl, sir.'

This was one of the differences between the three of us and our new friend. We were essentially taking the piss, except when we were serious. He was essentially serious, except when he was taking the piss. It took us a while to work this out.

Adrian allowed himself to be absorbed into our group, without acknowledging that it was something he sought. Perhaps he didn't. Nor did he alter his views to accord with ours. At morning prayers he could be heard joining in the responses while Alex and I merely mimed the words, and Colin preferred the satirical ploy of the pseudo-zealot's enthusiastic bellow. The three of us considered school sports a crypto-fascist plan for repressing our sex-drive; Adrian joined the fencing club and did the high jump. We were belligerently tone-deaf; he came to school with his clarinet. When Colin denounced the family, I mocked the political system, and Alex made philosophical objections to the perceived nature of reality, Adrian kept his counsel – at first, anyway. He gave the impression that he believed in things. We did too – it was just that we wanted to believe in our own things, rather than what had been decided for us. Hence what we thought of as our cleansing scepticism.

The school was in central London, and each day we travelled up to it from our separate boroughs, passing from one system of control to another. Back then, things were plainer: less money, no electronic devices, little fashion tyranny, no girlfriends. There was nothing to distract us from our human and filial duty which was to study, pass exams, use those qualifications to find a job, and then put together a way of life unthreateningly fuller than that of our parents, who would approve, while privately comparing it to their own earlier lives, which had been simpler, and therefore superior. None of this, of course, was ever stated: the genteel social Darwinism of the English middle classes always remained implicit.

'Fucking bastards, parents,' Colin complained one Monday lunchtime. 'You think they're OK when you're little, then you realise they're just like . . .'

'Henry VIII, Col?' Adrian suggested. We were beginning to get used to his sense of irony; also to the fact that it might be turned against us as well. When teasing, or calling us to seriousness, he would address me as Anthony; Alex would become Alexander, and the unlengthenable Colin shortened to Col.

'Wouldn't mind if my dad had half a dozen wives.'

'And was incredibly rich.'

'And painted by Holbein.'

'And told the Pope to sod off.'

'Any particular reason why they're FBs?' Alex asked Colin.

'I wanted us to go to the funfair. They said they had to spend the weekend gardening.'

Right: fucking bastards. Except to Adrian, who listened to our denunciations, but rarely joined in. And yet, it seemed to us, he had more cause than most. His mother had walked out years before, leaving his dad to cope with Adrian and his sister. This was long before the term 'single-parent family' came into use; back then it was 'a broken home', and Adrian was the only person we knew who came from one. This ought to have given him a whole storetank of existential rage, but somehow it didn't; he said he loved his mother and respected his father. Privately, the three of us examined his case and came up with a theory: that the key to a happy family life was for there not to be a family – or at least, not one living together. Having made this analysis, we envied Adrian the more.

In those days, we imagined ourselves as being kept in some kind of holding pen, waiting to be released into our lives. And when that moment came, our lives – and time itself – would speed up. How were we to know that our lives had in any case begun, that some advantage had already been gained, some damage already inflicted? Also, that our release would only be into a larger holding pen, whose boundaries would be at first undiscernible.

In the meantime, we were book-hungry, sex-hungry, meritocratic, anarchistic. All political and social systems appeared to us corrupt, yet we declined to consider an alternative other than hedonistic chaos. Adrian, however, pushed us to believe in the application of thought to life, in the notion that principles should guide actions. Previously, Alex had been regarded as the philosopher among us. He had read stuff the other two hadn't, and might, for instance, suddenly declare, 'Whereof we cannot speak, thereof must we remain silent.' Colin and I would consider this idea in silence for a while, then grin and carry on talking. But now Adrian's arrival dislodged Alex from his position – or rather, gave us another choice of philosopher. If Alex had read Russell and Wittgenstein, Adrian had read Camus and

Nietzsche. I had read George Orwell and Aldous Huxley; Colin had read Baudelaire and Dostoevsky. This is only a slight caricature.

Yes, of course we were pretentious – what else is youth for? We used terms like '*Weltanschauung*' and '*Sturm und Drang*', enjoyed saying 'That's philosophically self-evident', and assured one another that the imagination's first duty was to be transgressive. Our parents saw things differently, picturing their children as innocents suddenly exposed to noxious influence. So Colin's mother referred to me as his 'dark angel'; my father blamed Alex when he found me reading *The Communist Manifesto*; Colin was fingered by Alex's parents when they caught him with a hard-boiled American crime novel. And so on. It was the same with sex. Our parents thought we might be corrupted by one another into becoming whatever it was they most feared: an incorrigible masturbator, a winsome homosexual, a recklessly impregnatory libertine. On our behalf they dreaded the closeness of adolescent friendship, the predatory behaviour of strangers on trains, the lure of the wrong kind of girl. How far their anxieties outran our experience.

One afternoon Old Joe Hunt, as if picking up Adrian's earlier challenge, asked us to debate the origins of the First World War: specifically, the responsibility of Archduke Franz Ferdinand's assassin for starting the whole thing off. Back then, we were most of us absolutists. We liked Yes v No, Praise v Blame, Guilt v Innocence – or, in Marshall's case, Unrest v Great Unrest. We liked a game that ended in a win and loss, not a draw. And so for some, the Serbian gunman, whose name is long gone from my memory, had one hundred per cent individual responsibility: take him out of the equation, and the war would never have happened. Others preferred the one hundred per cent responsibility of historical forces, which had placed the antagonistic nations on an inevitable collision course: 'Europe was a powder keg waiting to blow', and so on. The more anarchic, like Colin, argued that everything was down to chance, that the world existed in a state of perpetual chaos, and only some primitive storytelling instinct, itself doubtless a hangover from religion, retrospectively imposed meaning on what might or might not have happened.

Hunt gave a brief nod to Colin's attempt to undermine everything, as if morbid disbelief was a natural by-product of adolescence, something to be grown out of. Masters and parents used to remind us irritatingly that they too had once been young, and so could speak with authority. It's just a phase, they would insist. You'll grow out of it; life will teach you reality and realism. But back then we declined to acknowledge that they had ever been anything like us, and we knew that we grasped life – and truth, and morality, and art – far more clearly than our compromised elders.

'Finn, you've been quiet. You started this ball rolling. You are, as it were, our Serbian gunman.' Hunt paused to let the allusion take effect. 'Would you care to give us the benefit of your thoughts?'

'I don't know, sir.'

'What don't you know?'

'Well, in one sense, I can't know what it is that I don't know. That's philosophically self-evident.' He left one of those slight pauses in which we again wondered if he was engaged in subtle mockery or a high seriousness beyond the rest of us. 'Indeed, isn't the whole business of ascribing responsibility a kind of cop-out? We want to blame an individual so that everyone else is exculpated. Or we blame a historical process as a way of exonerating individuals. Or it's all anarchic chaos, with the same consequence. It seems to me that there is – was – a chain of individual responsibilities, all of which were necessary, but not so long a chain that everybody can simply blame everyone else. But of course, my desire to ascribe responsibility might be more a reflection of my own cast of mind than a fair analysis of what happened. That's one of the central problems of history, isn't it, sir? The question of subjective versus objective interpretation, the fact that we need to know the history of the historian in order to understand the version that is being put in front of us.'

There was a silence. And no, he wasn't taking the piss, not in the slightest.

Old Joe Hunt looked at his watch and smiled. 'Finn, I retire in five years. And I shall be happy to give you a reference if you care to take over.' And he wasn't taking the piss either.

At assembly one morning, the headmaster, in the sombre voice he kept for expulsions and catastrophic sporting defeats, announced that he was the bearer of grievous news, namely that Robson of the Science Sixth had passed away during the weekend. Over a susurrus of awed mutterings, he told us that Robson had been cut down in the flower of youth, that his demise was a loss to the whole school, and that we would all be symbolically present at the funeral. Everything, in fact, except what we wanted to know: how, and why, and if it turned out to be murder, by whom.

'Eros and Thanatos,' Adrian commented before the day's first lesson. 'Thanatos wins again.'

'Robson wasn't exactly Eros-and-Thanatos material,' Alex told him. Colin and I nodded agreement. We knew because he'd been in our class for a couple of years: a steady, unimaginative boy, gravely uninterested in the arts, who had trundled along without offending anyone. Now he had offended us by making a name for himself with an early death. The flower of youth, indeed: the Robson we had known was vegetable matter.

There was no mention of disease, a bicycling accident or a gas explosion, and a few days later rumour (aka Brown of the Maths Sixth) supplied what the authorities couldn't, or wouldn't. Robson had got his girlfriend pregnant, hanged himself in the attic, and not been found for two days.

'I'd never have thought he knew how to hang himself.'

'He was in the Science Sixth.'

'But you need a special sort of slip knot.'

'That's only in films. And proper executions. You can do it with an ordinary knot. Just takes longer to suffocate you.'

'What do we think his girlfriend's like?'

We considered the options known to us: prim virgin (now ex-virgin), tarty shopgirl, experienced older woman, VD-riddled whore. We discussed this until Adrian redirected our interests.

'Camus said that suicide was the only true philosophical question.'

'Apart from ethics and politics and aesthetics and the

nature of reality and all the other stuff.' There was an edge to Alex's riposte.

'The only *true* one. The fundamental one on which all others depend.'

After a long analysis of Robson's suicide, we concluded that it could only be considered philosophical in an arithmetical sense of the term: he, being about to cause an increase of one in the human population, had decided it was his ethical duty to keep the planet's numbers constant. But in all other respects we judged that Robson had let us – and serious thinking – down. His action had been unphilosophical, self-indulgent and inartistic: in other words, wrong. As for his suicide note, which according to rumour (Brown again) read 'Sorry, Mum', we felt that it had missed a powerful educative opportunity.

Perhaps we wouldn't have been so hard on Robson if it hadn't been for one central, unshiftable fact: Robson was our age, he was in our terms unexceptional, and yet he had not only conspired to find a girlfriend but also, incontestably, to have had sex with her. Fucking bastard! Why him and not us? Why had none of us even had the experience of *failing* to get a girlfriend? At least the humiliation of that would have added to our general wisdom, given us something to negatively boast about ('Actually, "pustular berk with the charisma of a plimsole" were her exact words'). We knew from our reading of great literature that Love involved Suffering, and would happily have got in some practice at Suffering if there was an implicit, perhaps even logical, promise that Love might be on its way.

This was another of our fears: that Life wouldn't turn out to be like Literature. Look at our parents – were they the stuff of Literature? At best, they might aspire to the condition of onlookers and bystanders, part of a social backdrop against which real, true, important things could happen. Like what? The things Literature was all about: love, sex, morality, friendship, happiness, suffering, betrayal, adultery, good and evil, heroes and villains, guilt and innocence, ambition, power, justice, revolution, war, fathers and sons, mothers and daughters, the individual against society, success and failure, murder, suicide, death, God. And barn owls. Of course, there were other sorts of literature – theoretical, self-referential, lachrymosely autobiographical – but they were just dry wanks. Real literature was about psychological, emotional and social truth as demonstrated by the actions and reflections of its protagonists; the novel was about character developed over time. That's what Phil Dixon had told us anyway. And the only person – apart from Robson – whose life so far contained anything remotely novel-worthy was Adrian.

'Why did your mum leave your dad?'

'I'm not sure.'

'Did your mum have another bloke?'

'Was your father a cuckold?'

'Did your dad have a mistress?'

'I don't know. They said I'd understand when I was older.'

'That's what they always promise. How about explaining it *now*, that's what I say.' Except that I never had said this. And our house, as far as I could tell, contained no mysteries, to my shame and disappointment.

'Maybe your mum has a young lover?'

'How would I know. We never meet there. She always comes up to London.'

This was hopeless. In a novel, Adrian wouldn't just have accepted things as they were put to him. What was the point of having a situation worthy of fiction if the protagonist didn't behave as he would have done in a book? Adrian should have gone snooping, or saved up his pocket money and employed a private detective; perhaps all four of us should have gone off on a Quest to Discover the Truth. Or would that have been less like literature and too much like a kids' story?

In our final history lesson of the year, Old Joe Hunt, who had guided his lethargic pupils through Tudors and Stuarts, Victorians and Edwardians, the Rise of Empire and its Subsequent Decline, invited us to look back over all those centuries and attempt to draw conclusions.

'We could start, perhaps, with the seemingly simple question, What is History? Any thoughts, Webster?'

'History is the lies of the victors,' I replied, a little too quickly.

'Yes, I was rather afraid you'd say that. Well, as long as you remember that it is also the self-delusions of the defeated. Simpson?'

Colin was more prepared than me. 'History is a raw onion sandwich, sir.'

'For what reason?'

'It just repeats, sir. It burps. We've seen it again and again this year. Same old story, same old oscillation between tyranny and rebellion, war and peace, prosperity and impoverishment.'

'Rather a lot for a sandwich to contain, wouldn't you say?'

We laughed far more than was required, with an end-of-term hysteria.

'Finn?'

'"History is that certainty produced at the point where the imperfections of memory meet the inadequacies of documentation."'

'Is it, indeed? Where did you find that?'

'Lagrange, sir. Patrick Lagrange. He's French.'

'So one might have guessed. Would you care to give us an example?'

'Robson's suicide, sir.'

There was a perceptible intake of breath and some reckless head-turning. But Hunt, like the other masters, allowed Adrian special status. When the rest of us tried provocation, it was dismissed as puerile cynicism – something else we would grow out of. Adrian's provocations were somehow welcomed as awkward searchings after truth.

'What has that to do with the matter?'

'It's a historical event, sir, if a minor one. But recent. So it ought to be easily understood as history. We know that he's dead, we know that he had a girlfriend, we know that she's pregnant – or was. What else do we have? A single piece of documentation, a suicide note reading "Sorry, Mum" – at least, according to Brown. Does that note still exist? Was it destroyed? Did Robson have any other motives or reasons beyond the obvious ones? What was his state of mind? Can we be sure the child was his? We can't know, sir, not even this soon afterwards. So how might anyone write Robson's story in fifty years' time, when his parents are dead and his girlfriend has disappeared and doesn't want to remember him anyway? You see the problem, sir?'

We all looked at Hunt, wondering if Adrian had pushed it too far this time. That single word 'pregnant' seemed to hover like chalk-dust. And as for the audacious suggestion of alternative paternity, of Robson the Schoolboy Cuckold . . . After a while, the master replied.

'I see the problem, Finn. But I think you underestimate history. And for that matter historians. Let us assume for the sake of argument that poor Robson were to prove of historical interest. Historians have always been faced with the lack of direct evidence for things. That's what they're used to. And don't forget that in the present case there would have been an inquest, and therefore a coroner's report. Robson may well have kept a diary, or written letters, made phone calls whose contents are remembered. His parents would have replied to the letters of condolence they received. And fifty years from now, given the current life expectancy, quite a few of his schoolfellows would still be available for interview. The problem might be less daunting than you imagine.'

'But nothing can make up for the absence of Robson's testimony, sir.'

'In one way, no. But equally, historians need to treat a participant's own explanation of events with a certain scepticism. It is often the statement made with an eye to the future that is the most suspect.'

'If you say so, sir.'

'And mental states may often be inferred from actions. The tyrant rarely sends a handwritten note requesting the elimination of an enemy.'

'If you say so, sir.'

'Well, I do.'

Was this their exact exchange? Almost certainly not. Still, it is my best memory of their exchange.

We finished school, promised lifelong friendship, and went our separate ways. Adrian, to nobody's surprise, won a scholarship to Cambridge. I read history at Bristol; Colin went to Sussex, and Alex into his father's business. We wrote letters to one another, as people – even the young – did in those days. But we had little experience of the form, so an arch self-consciousness often preceded any urgency of content. To start a letter, 'Being in receipt of your epistle of the 17th inst' seemed, for some while, quite witty.

We swore to meet every time the three of us at university came home for the vacation; yet it didn't always work out. And writing to one another seemed to have recalibrated the dynamics of our relationship. The original three wrote less often and less enthusiastically to one another than we did to Adrian. We wanted his attention, his approval; we courted him, and told him our best stories first; we each thought we were – and deserved to be – closest to him. And though we were making new friends ourselves, we were somehow persuaded that Adrian wasn't: that we three were still his nearest intimates, that he depended on us. Was this just to disguise the fact that we were dependent on him?

And then life took over, and time speeded up. In other words, I found a girlfriend. Of course, I'd met a few girls before, but either their self-assurance made me feel gauche, or their nervousness compounded my own. There was, apparently, some secret masculine code, handed down from suave twenty-year-olds to tremulous eighteen-year-olds, which, once mastered, enabled you to 'pick up' girls and, in certain circumstances, 'get off' with them. But I never learnt or understood it, and probably still don't. My 'technique' consisted in not having a technique; others, no doubt rightly, considered it ineptitude. Even the supposedly simple trail of like-a-drink-fancy-a-dance-walk-you-home-how-about-a-coffee? involved a bravado I was incapable of. I just hung around and tried to make interesting remarks while expecting to mess things up. I remember feeling sad through drink at a party in my first term, and when a passing girl asked sympathetically if I was OK, I found myself replying, 'I think I'm a manic depressive,' because at the time it felt more characterful than 'I'm feeling a bit sad.' When she replied, 'Not another,' and moved swiftly on, I realised that, far from making myself stand out from the cheery crowd, I had attempted the world's worst pick-up line.

My girlfriend was called Veronica Mary Elizabeth Ford, information (by which I mean her middle names) it took me two months to extract. She was reading Spanish, she liked poetry, and her father was a civil servant. About five foot two with rounded, muscular calves, mid-brown hair to her shoulders, blue-grey eyes behind blue-framed spectacles, and a quick yet withholding smile. I thought she was nice. Well, I probably would have found any girl who didn't shy away from me nice. I didn't try telling her I felt sad because I didn't. She owned a Black Box record player to my Dansette, and had better musical taste: that's to say, she despised Dvořák and Tchaikovsky, whom I adored, and owned some choral and lieder LPs. She looked through my record collection with an occasional flickering smile and a more frequent frown. The fact that I'd hidden both the 1812 Overture and the soundtrack to *Un Homme et Une Femme* didn't spare me. There was enough dubious material even before she reached my extensive pop section: Elvis, the Beatles, the Stones (not that anyone could object to them, surely), but also the Hollies, the Animals, the Moody Blues and a two-disc boxed set of Donovan called (in lower case) *a gift from a flower to a garden*.

'You like this stuff?' she asked neutrally.

'Good to dance to,' I replied, a little defensively.

'Do you dance to it? Here? In your room? By yourself?'

'No, not really.' Though of course I did.

'I don't dance,' she said, part anthropologist, part layer-down of rules for any relationship we might have, were we to go out together.

I'd better explain what the concept of 'going out' with someone meant back then, because time has changed it. I was talking recently to a woman friend whose daughter had come to her in a state of distress. She was in her second term at university, and had been sleeping with a boy who had – openly, and to her knowledge – been sleeping with several other girls at the same time. What he was doing was auditioning them all before deciding which to 'go out' with. The daughter was upset, not so much by the system – though she half-perceived its injustice – as by the fact that she hadn't been the one finally chosen.

This made me feel like a survivor from some antique, bypassed culture whose members were still using carved turnips as a form of monetary exchange. Back in 'my day' – though I didn't claim ownership of it at the time, still less do I now – this is what used to happen: you met a girl, you were attracted to her, you tried to ingratiate yourself, you would invite her to a couple of social events – for instance, the pub – then ask her out on her own, then again, and after a goodnight kiss of variable heat, you were somehow, officially, 'going out' with her. Only when you were semi-publicly committed did you discover what her sexual policy might be. And sometimes this meant her body would be as tightly guarded as a fisheries exclusion zone.

Veronica wasn't very different from other girls of the time. They were physically comfortable with you, took your arm in public, kissed you until the colour rose, and might consciously press their breasts against you as long as there were about five layers of clothing between flesh and flesh. They would be perfectly aware of what was going on in your trousers without ever mentioning it. And that was all, for quite a while. Some girls allowed more: you heard of those who went in for mutual masturbation, others who permitted 'full sex', as it was known. You couldn't appreciate the gravity of that 'full' unless you'd had a lot of the half-empty kind. And then, as the relationship continued, there were certain implicit trade-offs, some based on whim, others on promise and commitment – up to what the poet called 'a wrangle for a ring'.

Subsequent generations might be inclined to put all this down to religion or prudery. But the girls – or women – with whom I had what might be called infra-sex (yes, it wasn't only Veronica) were at ease with their bodies. And, if certain criteria obtained, with mine. I don't mean to suggest, by the way, that infra-sex was unexciting, or even, except in the obvious way, frustrating. Besides, these girls were allowing far more than their mothers had, and I was getting far more than my father had done. At least, so

I presumed. And anything was better than nothing. Except that, in the meantime, Colin and Alex had fixed themselves up with girlfriends who didn't have any exclusion-zone policies – or so their hints implied. But then, no one told the whole truth about sex. And in that respect, nothing has changed.

I wasn't exactly a virgin, just in case you were wondering. Between school and university I had a couple of instructive episodes, whose excitements were greater than the mark they left. So what happened subsequently made me feel all the odder: the more you liked a girl, and the better matched you were, the less your chance of sex, it seemed. Unless, of course – and this is a thought I didn't articulate until later – something in me was attracted to women who said no. But can such a perverse instinct exist?

'Why not?' you would ask, as a restraining hand was clamped to your wrist.

'It doesn't feel right.'

This was an exchange heard in front of many a breathy gas fire, counterpointed by many a whistling kettle. And there was no arguing against 'feelings', because women were experts in them, men coarse beginners. So 'It doesn't feel right' had far more persuasive force and irrefutability than any appeal to church doctrine or a mother's advice. You may say, But wasn't this the Sixties? Yes, but only for some people, only in certain parts of the country.

My bookshelves were more successful with Veronica than my record collection. In those days, paperbacks came in their traditional liveries: orange Penguins for fiction, blue Pelicans for non-fiction. To have more blue than orange on your shelf was proof of seriousness. And overall, I had enough of the right titles: Richard Hoggart, Steven Runciman, Huizinga, Eysenck, Empson . . . plus Bishop John Robinson's *Honest to God* next to my Larry cartoon books. Veronica paid me the compliment of assuming I'd read them all, and didn't suspect that the most worn titles had been bought second-hand.

Her own shelves held a lot of poetry, in volume and pamphlet form: Eliot, Auden, MacNeice, Stevie Smith, Thom Gunn, Ted Hughes. There were Left Book Club editions of Orwell and Koestler, some calf-bound nineteenth-century novels, a couple of childhood Arthur Rackhams, and her comfort book, *I Capture the Castle*. I didn't for a moment doubt that she had read them all, or that they were the right books to own. Further, they seemed to be an organic continuation of her mind and personality, whereas mine struck me as functionally separate, straining to describe a character I hoped to grow into. This disparity threw me into a slight panic, and as I looked along her poetry shelf I fell back on a line of Phil Dixon's.

'Of course, everyone's wondering what Ted Hughes will do when he runs out of animals.'

'Are they?'

'So I've been told,' I said feebly. In Dixon's mouth, the line had seemed witty and sophisticated; in mine, merely facetious.

'Poets don't run out of material the way novelists do,' she instructed me. 'Because they don't depend on material in the same way. And you're treating him like a sort of zoologist, aren't you? But even zoologists don't tire of animals, do they?'

She was looking at me with one eyebrow raised above

the frame of her glasses. She was five months older than me and sometimes made it feel like five years.

'It was just something my English master said.'

'Well, now you're at university we must get you to think for yourself, mustn't we?'

There was something about the 'we' that made me suspect I hadn't got everything wrong. She was just trying to improve me – and who was I to object to that? One of the first things she asked me was why I wore my watch on the inside of my wrist. I couldn't justify it, so I turned the face round, and put time on the outside, as normal, grown-up people did.

I settled into a contented routine of working, spending my free time with Veronica and, back in my student room, wanking explosively to fantasies of her splayed beneath me or arched above me. Daily intimacy made me proud of knowing about make-up, clothes policy, the feminine razor, and the mystery and consequences of a woman's periods. I found myself envying this regular reminder of something so wholly female and defining, so connected to the great cycle of nature. I may have put it as badly as this when I tried to explain the feeling.

'You're just romanticising what you haven't got. The only point of it is to tell you you're not pregnant.'

Given our relationship, this struck me as a bit cheeky.

'Well, I hope we're not living in Nazareth.'

There followed one of those pauses when couples tacitly agree not to discuss something. And what was there to discuss? Only, perhaps, the unwritten terms of the trade-off. From my point of view, the fact that we weren't having sex exonerated me from thinking about the relationship other than as a close complicity with a woman who, as her part of the bargain, wasn't going to ask the man where the relationship was heading. At least, that's what I thought the deal was. But I was wrong about most things, then as now. For instance, why did I assume she was a virgin? I never asked her, and she never told me. I assumed she was because she wouldn't sleep with me: and where is the logic in that?

One weekend in the vacation, I was invited to meet her family. They lived in Kent, out on the Orpington line, in one of those suburbs which had stopped concreting over nature at the very last minute, and ever since smugly claimed rural status. On the train down from Charing Cross, I worried that my suitcase – the only one I owned – was so large it made me look like a potential burglar. At the station, Veronica introduced me to her father, who opened the boot of his car, took the suitcase from my hand, and laughed.

'Looks like you're planning to move in, young man.'

He was large, fleshy and red-faced; he struck me as gross. Was that beer on his breath? At this time of day? How could this man have fathered such an elfin daughter?

He drove his Humber Super Snipe with a sighing impatience at the folly of others. I sat in the back, alone. Occasionally, he would point things out, presumably to me, though I couldn't tell if I was meant to reply. 'St Michael's, brick and flint, much improved by Victorian restorers.' 'Our very own Café Royal – *voilà!*' 'Note the distinguished off-licence with period half-timbering on your right.' I looked at Veronica's profile for a clue, but received none.

They lived in a detached, red-brick, tile-hung house

with a strip of gravel in front of it. Mr Ford opened the front door and shouted to no one in particular,

'The boy's come for a month.'

I noticed the heavy shine on the dark furniture, and the heavy shine on the leaves of an extravagant pot plant. Veronica's father seized my case as if responding to the distant laws of hospitality and, farcically exaggerating its weight, carried it up to an attic room and threw it on the bed. He pointed to a small plumbed-in basin.

'Pee in there in the night if you want to.'

I nodded in reply. I couldn't tell if he was being all matily male, or treating me as lower-class scum.

Veronica's brother, Jack, was easier to read: one of those healthy, sporting young men who laughed at most things and teased his younger sister. He behaved towards me as if I were an object of mild curiosity, and by no means the first to be exhibited for his appreciation. Veronica's mother ignored all the by-play around her, asked me about my studies, and disappeared into the kitchen a lot. I suppose she must have been in her early forties, though of course she appeared to me deep into middle age, as did her husband. She didn't look much like Veronica: a broader face, hair tied off her high forehead with a ribbon, a bit more than average height. She had a somewhat artistic air, though precisely how this expressed itself – colourful scarves, a distrait manner, the humming of opera arias, or all three – I couldn't at this distance testify.

I was so ill at ease that I spent the entire weekend constipated: this is my principal factual memory. The rest consists of impressions and half-memories which may therefore be self-serving: for instance, how Veronica, despite having invited me down, seemed at first to withdraw into her family and join in their examination of me – though whether this was the cause, or the consequence, of my insecurity, I can't from here determine. Over supper that Friday there was some questioning of my social and intellectual credentials; I felt as if I were before a court of inquiry. Afterwards we watched the TV news and awkwardly discussed world affairs until bedtime. Had we been in a novel, there might have been some sneaking between floors for a hot cuddle after the paterfamilias had locked up for the night. But we weren't; Veronica didn't even kiss me goodnight that first evening, or make some excuse about towels, and seeing I had everything I needed. Perhaps she feared her brother's mockery. So I undressed, washed, peed aggressively in the basin, got into my pyjamas and lay awake for a long time.

When I came down for breakfast, only Mrs Ford was around. The others had gone for a walk, Veronica having assured everyone that I would want to sleep in. I can't have disguised my reaction to this very well, as I could sense Mrs Ford examining me while she made bacon and eggs, frying things in a slapdash way and breaking one of the yolks. I wasn't experienced at talking to girlfriends' mothers.

'Have you lived here long?' I eventually asked, though I already knew the answer.

She paused, poured herself a cup of tea, broke another egg into the pan, leant back against a dresser stacked with plates, and said,

'Don't let Veronica get away with too much.'

I didn't know how to reply. Should I be offended at

this interference in our relationship, or fall into confessional mode and 'discuss' Veronica? So I said, a little primly,

'What do you mean, Mrs Ford?'

She looked at me, smiled in an unpatronising way, shook her head slightly, and said, 'We've lived here ten years.'

So in the end I was almost as much at sea with her as with the rest of them, though at least she appeared to like me. She eased another egg on to my plate, despite my not asking for it or wanting it. The remnants of the broken one were still in the pan; she flipped them casually into the swing-bin, then half-threw the hot frying pan into the wet sink. Water fizzed and steam rose at the impact, and she laughed, as if she had enjoyed causing this small havoc.

When Veronica and the menfolk returned, I was expecting further examination, perhaps even some trick or game; instead there were polite enquiries after my sleep and comfort. This ought to have made me feel accepted, but it seemed more as if they had grown tired of me, and the weekend was now just something to be got through. Perhaps this was mere paranoia. But on the plus side, Veronica became more openly affectionate; over tea she was happy to put her hand on my arm and fiddle with my hair. At one point, she turned to her brother and said,

'He'll do, won't he?'

Jack winked at me; I didn't wink back. Instead, part of me felt like stealing some towels, or walking mud into the carpet.

Still, things were mostly almost normal. That evening, Veronica walked me upstairs and kissed me goodnight properly. For Sunday lunch there was a joint of roast lamb with enormous sprigs of rosemary sticking out of it like bits of Christmas tree. Since my parents had taught me manners, I said how delicious it was. Then I caught Jack winking at his father, as if to say: What a creep. But Mr Ford chortled, 'Hear, hear, motion seconded,' while Mrs Ford thanked me.

When I came downstairs to say goodbye, Mr Ford seized my suitcase and said to his wife, 'I trust you've counted the spoons, darling?' She didn't bother to answer, just smiled at me, almost as if we had a secret. Brother Jack didn't show up to say farewell; Veronica and her father got into the front of the car; I sat in the back again. Mrs Ford was leaning against the porch, sunlight falling on a wisteria climbing the house above her head. As Mr Ford put the car into gear and spun the wheels on the gravel, I waved goodbye, and she responded, though not the way people normally do, with a raised palm, but with a sort of horizontal gesture at waist level. I rather wished I'd talked to her more.

To stop Mr Ford pointing out the wonders of Chislehurst a second time, I said to Veronica, 'I like your mum.'

'Sounds like you've got a rival, Vron,' said Mr Ford, with a theatrical intake of breath. 'Come to think of it, sounds like I have too. Pistols at dawn, young feller-me-lad?'

My train was late, slowed by the usual Sunday engineering work. I got home in the early evening. I remember that I had a bloody good long shit.

A week or so later, Veronica came up to town so I could introduce her to my gang from school. It proved an aimless day of which no one wanted to take charge. We went round the Tate, then walked up to Buckingham Palace and into Hyde Park, heading for Speakers' Corner. But there weren't any speakers in action, so we wandered along Oxford Street looking at the shops, and ended up in Trafalgar Square among the lions. Anyone would have thought we were tourists.

At first I was watching to see how my friends reacted to Veronica, but soon became more interested in what she thought of them. She laughed at Colin's jokes more easily than at mine, which annoyed me, and asked Alex how his father made his money (marine insurance, he told her, to my surprise). She seemed happy to keep Adrian for last. I'd told her he was at Cambridge, and she tried out various names on him. At a couple of them he nodded and said,

'Yes, I know the sort of people they are.'

This sounded pretty rude to me, but Veronica didn't take offence. Instead, she mentioned colleges and dons and tea shops in a way that made me feel left out.

'How come you know so much about the place?' I asked.

'That's where Jack is.'

'Jack?'

'My brother – you remember?'

'Let me see . . . Was he the one who was younger than your father?'

I thought that wasn't bad, but she didn't even smile.

'What's Jack reading?' I asked, trying to make up ground.

'Moral sciences,' she replied. 'Like Adrian.'

I know what Adrian's bloody reading, thank you very much, I wanted to say. Instead I sulked for a while, and talked to Colin about films.

Towards the end of the afternoon we took photos; she asked for 'one with your friends'. The three of them shuffled politely into line, whereupon she rearranged them: Adrian and Colin, the two tallest, on either side of her, with Alex beyond Colin. The resulting print made her look even slighter than she did in the flesh. Many years later, when I came to examine this photo again, looking for answers, I wondered about the fact that she never wore heels of any height. I'd read somewhere that if you want to make people pay attention to what you're saying, you don't raise your voice but lower it: this is what really commands attention. Perhaps hers was a similar kind of trick with height. Though whether she went in for tricks is a question I still haven't resolved. When I was going out with her, it always seemed that her actions were instinctive. But then I was resistant to the whole idea that women were or could be manipulative. This may tell you more about me than it does about her. And even if I were to decide, at this late stage, that she was and always had been calculating, I'm not sure it would help matters. By which I mean: help me.

We walked her to Charing Cross and waved her off to Chislehurst in a mock-heroic way, as if she were travelling to Samarkand. Then we sat in the bar of the station hotel, drinking beer and feeling very grown up.

'Nice girl,' said Colin.

'Very nice,' added Alex.

'That's philosophically self-evident!' I almost shouted. Well, I was a little overexcited. I turned to Adrian. 'Any advance on "very nice"?'

'You don't actually need me to congratulate you, do you, Anthony?'

'Yes, why the fuck shouldn't I?'

'Then of course I do.'

But his attitude seemed to criticise my neediness and the other two for pandering to it. I felt slightly panicked;

I didn't want the day to unravel. Though looking back, it was not the day, but the four of us, that were beginning to unravel.

'So, have you come across Brother Jack at Cambridge?'

'I haven't met him, no, and don't expect to. He's in his final year. But I've heard of him, read about him in a magazine article. And about the people he goes around with, yes.'

He clearly wanted to leave it at that, but I wouldn't let him.

'And so what do you think of him?'

Adrian paused. He took a sip of beer, and then said with sudden vehemence, 'I *hate* the way the English have of not being serious about being serious. I *really hate* it.'

In another mood, I might have taken this as a strike against the three of us. Instead, I felt a throb of vindication.

Veronica and I continued going out together, all through our second year. One evening, perhaps a little drunk, she let me put my hand down her knickers. I felt extravagant pride as I scuffled around. She wouldn't let me put my finger inside her, but wordlessly, over the next days, we developed a way to pleasure. We would be on the floor, kissing. I would take off my watch, roll up my left sleeve, put my hand into her knickers and gradually shuffle them down her thighs a little; then I would place my hand flat on the floor, and she would rub herself against my trapped wrist until she came. For a few weeks this made me feel masterful, but back in my room my wanking was sometimes edged with resentment. And what kind of a trade-off had I got myself into now? A better, or a worse one? I discovered something else I couldn't understand: I was, presumably, meant to feel closer to her, but didn't.

'So, do you ever think about where our relationship is heading?'

She said it just like that, out of the blue. She had come round for tea, bringing slices of fruitcake.

'Do you?'

'I asked first.'

I thought – and it may not have been a gallant reaction – is this why you started letting me put my hand down your pants?

'Does it have to head somewhere?'

'Isn't that what relationships do?'

'I don't know. I haven't been in enough of them.'

'Look, Tony,' she said. 'I don't stagnate.'

I thought about this for a while, or tried to. But instead kept seeing an image of stagnant water, with thick scum and hovering mosquitoes. I realised I wasn't much good at discussing this sort of stuff.

'So you think we're stagnating?'

She did that eyebrow-above-the-spectacle-frame tic that I no longer found quite so cute. I went on,

'Isn't there something between stagnation and heading somewhere?'

'Like?'

'Like having a nice time. Enjoy the day and all that?' But just saying this made me wonder if I *was* enjoying the day any longer. I also thought: What does she want me to say?

'And do you think we're suited?'

'You keep asking me questions as if you know the answer to them. Or as if you know the answer you want.

· 34 ·

So why don't you tell me what it is and I'll tell you whether it's mine as well?'

'You're quite cowardly, aren't you, Tony?'

'I think it's more that I'm . . . peaceable.'

'Well, I wouldn't want to disturb your self-image.'

We finished our tea. I wrapped up the two remaining slices of cake and put them in a tin. Veronica kissed me nearer the corner of my lips than the centre, and then left. In my mind, this was the beginning of the end of our relationship. Or have I just remembered it this way to make it seem so, and to apportion blame? If asked in a court of law what happened and what was said, I could only attest to the words 'heading', 'stagnating' and 'peaceable'. I'd never thought of myself as peaceable – or its opposite – until then. I would also swear to the truth of the biscuit tin; it was burgundy red, with the Queen's smiling profile on it.

I don't want to give the impression that all I did at Bristol was work and see Veronica. But few other memories come back to me. One that does – one single, distinct event – was the night I witnessed the Severn Bore. The local paper used to print a timetable, indicating where best to catch it and when. But the first occasion I tried, the water didn't seem to be obeying its instructions. Then, one evening at Minsterworth, a group of us waited on the river bank until after midnight and were eventually rewarded. For an hour or two we observed the river flowing gently down to the sea as all good rivers do. The moon's intermittent lighting was assisted by the occasional explorations of a few powerful torches. Then there was a whisper, and a craning of necks, and all thoughts of damp and cold vanished as the river simply seemed to change its mind, and a wave, two or three feet high, was heading towards us, the water breaking across its whole width, from bank to bank. This heaving swell came level with us, surged past, and curved off into the distance; some of my mates gave chase, shouting and cursing and falling over as it outpaced them; I stayed on the bank by myself. I don't think I can properly convey the effect that moment had on me. It wasn't like a tornado or an earthquake (not that I'd witnessed either) – nature being violent and destructive, putting us in our place. It was more unsettling because it looked and felt quietly wrong, as if some small lever of the universe had been pressed, and here, just for these minutes, nature was reversed, and time with it. And to see this phenomenon after dark made it the more mysterious, the more other-worldly.

After we broke up, she slept with me.

Yes, I know. I expect you're thinking: The poor sap, how did he not see that coming? But I didn't. I thought we were over, and I thought there was another girl (a normal-sized girl who wore high heels to parties) I was interested in. I didn't see it coming at any point: when Veronica and I bumped into each other at the pub (she didn't like pubs), when she asked me to walk her home, when she stopped halfway there and we kissed, when we got to her room and I turned the light on and she turned it off again, when she took her knickers off and passed me a pack of Durex Fetherlite, or even when she took one from my fumbling hand and put it on me, or during the rest of the swift business.

Yes, you can say it again: You poor sap. And did you still think her a virgin when she was rolling a condom on to your cock? In a strange way, you know, I did. I thought it might be one of those intuitive female skills I inevitably lacked. Well, perhaps it was.

'You've got to hold on to it as you pull out,' she whispered (did she think *I* was a virgin, perhaps?). Then I got up and walked to the bathroom, the filled condom occasionally slapping against the inside of my thighs. As I disposed of it I came to a decision and a conclusion: No, it went, no.

'You selfish bastard,' she said, the next time we met.

'Yes, well, there it is.'

'That practically makes it rape.'

'I don't think anything at all makes it that.'

'Well, you might have had the decency to tell me beforehand.'

'I didn't know beforehand.'

'Oh, so it was that bad?'

'No, it was good. It's just . . .'

'Just what?'

'You were always asking me to think about our relationship and so now perhaps I have. I did.'

'Bravo. It must have been hard.'

I thought: And I haven't even seen her breasts, in all this time. Felt them, but not seen them. Also, she's completely wrong about Dvořák and Tchaikovsky. What's more, I'll be able to play my LP of *Un Homme et Une Femme* as often as I like. Openly.

'Sorry?'

'Jesus, Tony, you can't even concentrate *now*. My brother was right about you.'

I knew I was meant to ask what Brother Jack had said, but I didn't want to give her the pleasure. As I remained silent, she went on,

'And don't say that thing.'

Life seemed even more of a guessing game than usual.

'What thing?'

'About us still being able to be friends.'

'Is that what I'm meant to say?'

'You're meant to say what you *think*, what you *feel*, for Christ's sake, what you *mean*.'

'All right. In that case I won't say it – what I'm meant to say. Because I don't think we can still be friends.'

'Well done,' she said sarcastically. 'Well done.'

'But let me ask you a question then. Did you sleep with me to get me back?'

'I don't have to answer your questions any more.'

'In which case, why wouldn't you sleep with me when we were going out together?'

No answer.

'Because you didn't need to?'

'Perhaps I didn't want to.'

'Perhaps you didn't want to because you didn't need to.'

'Well, you can believe what it suits you to believe.'

The next day, I took a milk jug she'd given me down to the Oxfam shop. I hoped she'd see it in the window. But when I stopped to check, there was something else on show instead: a small coloured lithograph of Chislehurst I'd given her for Christmas.

At least we were studying different subjects, and Bristol was a large enough city for us only occasionally to half-run into one another. The times we did, I would be hit by a sense of what I can only call pre-guilt: the expectation that she was going to say or do something that would make me feel properly guilty. But she never deigned to speak to me, so this apprehension gradually wore off. And I told myself I didn't have anything to feel guilty about: we were both near-adults, responsible for our own actions, who had freely entered into a relationship which hadn't worked out. No one had got pregnant, no one had got killed.

In the second week of the summer vacation a letter arrived with a Chislehurst postmark. I inspected the unfamiliar handwriting – looping and slightly careless – on the envelope. A female hand: her mother, no doubt. Another burst of pre-guilt: perhaps Veronica had suffered a nervous collapse, become wasted and even more waiflike. Or perhaps she had peritonitis and was asking for me from her hospital bed. Or perhaps . . . but even I could tell these were self-important fantasies. The letter was indeed from Veronica's mother; it was brief and, to my surprise, not in the least accusatory. She was sorry to hear we had broken up, and sure I would find someone more suitable. But she didn't appear to mean this in the sense that I was a scoundrel who deserved someone of equally low moral character. Rather, she implied the opposite: that I was well out of things, and she hoped the best for me. I wish I'd kept that letter, because it would have been proof, corroboration. Instead, the only evidence comes from my memory – of a carefree, rather dashing woman who broke an egg, cooked me another, and told me not to take any shit from her daughter.

I went back to Bristol for my final year. The girl of normal height who wore heels was less interested than I'd imagined, and so I concentrated on work. I doubted I had the right kind of brain for a first, but was determined to get a 2:1. On Friday nights, I allowed myself the break of an evening at the pub. One time, a girl I'd been chatting to came back with me and stayed the night. It was all pleasantly exciting and effective, but neither of us contacted the other afterwards. I thought about this less at the time than I do now. I expect such recreational behaviour will strike later generations as quite unremarkable, both for nowadays and for back then: after all, wasn't 'back then' the Sixties? Yes it was, but as I said, it depended on where – and who – you were. If you'll excuse a brief history lesson: most people didn't experience 'the Sixties' until the Seventies. Which meant, logically, that most people in the Sixties were still experiencing the Fifties – or, in my case, bits of both decades side by side. Which made things rather confusing.

Logic: yes, where is logic? Where is it, for instance, in the next moment of my story? About halfway through my final year, I got a letter from Adrian. This had become an increasingly rare occurrence, as both of us were working hard for finals. He was of course expected to get a first. And then what? Postgraduate work, presumably, followed by academe, or some job in the public sphere where his brain and sense of responsibility would be put to good use. Someone once told me that the civil service (or at least, its higher echelons) was a fascinating place to work because you were always having to make moral decisions. Perhaps that would have suited Adrian. I certainly didn't see him as a worldly person, or an adventurous one – except intellectually, of course. He wasn't the sort who would get his name or face into the newspapers.

You can probably guess that I'm putting off telling

you the next bit. All right: Adrian said he was writing to ask my permission to go out with Veronica.

Yes, why her, and why then; furthermore, why ask? Actually, to be true to my own memory, as far as that's ever possible (and I didn't keep this letter either), what he said was that he and Veronica were already going out together, a state of affairs that would doubtless come to my attention sooner or later; and so it seemed better that I heard about it from him. Also, that while this news might come as a surprise, he hoped that I could understand and accept it, because if I couldn't, then he owed it to our friendship to reconsider his actions and decisions. And finally, that Veronica had agreed he should write this letter – indeed, it had been partly her suggestion.

As you can imagine, I enjoyed the bit about his moral scruples – implying that if I thought some venerable code of chivalry or, better still, some modern principle of ethics had been infringed, then he would, naturally and logically, stop fucking her. Assuming that she wasn't stringing him along as she had done me. I also liked the hypocrisy of a letter whose point was not just to tell me something I might not have found out anyway (or not for quite a while), but to let me know how she, Veronica, had traded up: to my cleverest friend, and, what's more, a Cambridge chap like Brother Jack. Also, to warn me that she would be hanging around if I planned on seeing Adrian – which had the desired effect of making me plan not to see Adrian. Pretty good for a day's work, or a night's. Again, I must stress that this is my reading now of what happened then. Or rather, my memory now of my reading then of what was happening at the time.

★

But I think I have an instinct for survival, for self-preservation. Perhaps this is what Veronica called cowardice and I called being peaceable. Anyway, something warned me not to get involved – at least, not now. I took the nearest postcard to hand – one of the Clifton Suspension Bridge – and wrote words like: 'Being in receipt of your epistle of the 21st, the undersigned begs to present his compliments and wishes to record that everything is jolly fine by me, old bean.' Silly, but unambiguous; and it would do for the moment. I would pretend – especially to myself – that I didn't mind in the slightest. I would study hard, put my emotions on hold, not take anyone home from the pub, masturbate as and when required, and make sure I got the degree I deserved. I did all that (and yes, I got a 2:1).

I stayed on for a few weeks after finishing my exams, fell in with a different group, drank systematically, smoked a bit of dope, and thought about very little. Apart from imagining what Veronica might have said to Adrian about me ('He took my virginity and then immediately dumped me. So really, the whole thing felt like rape, do you see?'). I imagined her buttering him up – I'd witnessed the start of that – and flattering him, playing on his expectations. As I said, Adrian was not a worldly person, for all his academic success. Hence the priggish tone of his letter, which for a while I used to reread with self-pitying frequency. When, at last, I replied to it properly, I didn't use any of that silly 'epistle' language. As far as I remember, I told him pretty much what I thought of their joint moral scruples. I also advised him to be prudent, because in my opinion Veronica had suffered damage a long way back. Then I wished him good luck, burnt his letter in an empty grate (melodramatic, I agree, but I plead youth as a mitigating circumstance), and decided that the two of them were now out of my life for ever.

What did I mean by 'damage'? It was only a guess; I didn't have any real evidence. But whenever I looked back on that unhappy weekend, I realised that it hadn't been just a matter of a rather naïve young man finding himself ill at ease among a posher and more socially skilled family. That was going on too, of course. But I could sense a complicity between Veronica and her heavy-footed, heavy-handed father, who treated me as substandard. Also between Veronica and Brother Jack, whose life and deportment she clearly regarded as nonpareil: he was the appointed judge when she asked publicly of me – and the question gets more condescending with each repetition – 'He'll do, won't he?' On the other hand, I saw no complicity at all with her mother, who doubtless recognised her for what she was. How did Mrs Ford have the initial chance to warn me against her daughter? Because that morning – the first morning after my arrival – Veronica had told everyone I wanted a lie-in, and gone off with her father and brother. No such exchange between us justified that invention. I never had lie-ins. I don't even have them now.

When I wrote to Adrian, I wasn't at all clear myself what I meant by 'damage'. And most of a lifetime later, I am only slightly clearer. My mother-in-law (who happily is not part of this story) didn't think much of me but was at least candid about it, as she was about most things. She once observed – when there was yet another case of child abuse filling the papers and television news reports – 'I reckon we were all abused.' Am I suggesting that Veronica was the victim of what they nowadays call 'inappropriate behaviour': beery leering from her father at bathtime or bedtime, something more than a sibling cuddle with her brother? How could I know? Was there some primal moment of loss, some withdrawal of love when it was most needed, some overheard exchange from which the child concluded that . . . ? Again, I cannot know. I have no evidence, anecdotal or documentary. But I remember what Old Joe Hunt said when arguing with Adrian: that mental states can be inferred from actions. That's in history – Henry VIII and all that. Whereas in the private life, I think the converse is true: that you can infer past actions from current mental states.

I certainly believe we all suffer damage, one way or another. How could we not, except in a world of perfect parents, siblings, neighbours, companions? And then there is the question, on which so much depends, of how we react to the damage: whether we admit it or repress it, and how this affects our dealings with others. Some admit the damage, and try to mitigate it; some spend their lives trying to help others who are damaged; and then there are those whose main concern is to avoid further damage to themselves, at whatever cost. And those are the ones who are ruthless, and the ones to be careful of.

You might think this is rubbish – preachy, self-justificatory rubbish. You might think that I behaved towards Veronica like a typically callow male, and that all my 'conclusions' are reversible. For instance, 'After we broke up, she slept with me' flips easily into 'After she slept with me, I broke up with her.' You might also decide that the Fords were a normal middle-class English family on whom I was chippily foisting bogus theories of damage; and that Mrs Ford, instead of being tactfully concerned on my behalf, was displaying an indecent jealousy of her own daughter. You might even ask me to apply my 'theory' to myself and explain what damage I had suffered a long way back and what its consequences might be: for instance, how it might affect my reliability and truthfulness. I'm not sure I could answer this, to be honest.

I didn't expect any reply from Adrian, nor did I get one. And now the prospect of seeing Colin and Alex by themselves became less appealing. Having been three, then four, how was it possible to go back to being three again? If the others wanted to make up their own party, fine, go ahead. I needed to get on with my life. So I did.

Some of my contemporaries did VSO, departing to Africa, where they taught schoolkids and built mud walls; I wasn't so high-minded. Also, back then you somehow assumed that a decent degree would ensure a decent job, sooner or later. 'Ti-*yi-yi-yime* is on my side, yes it is,' I used to yodel, duetting with Mick Jagger as I gyrated alone in my student room. So, leaving others to train as doctors and lawyers and sit the civil-service exams, I took myself off to the States and roamed around for six months. I waited on tables, painted fences, did gardening, and delivered cars across several states. In those years before mobile phones, email and Skype, travellers depended on the rudimentary communications system known as the postcard. Other methods – the long-distance phone call, the telegram – were marked 'For Emergency Use Only'. So my parents waved me off into the unknown, and their news bulletins about me would have been restricted to 'Yes, he's arrived safely', and 'Last time we heard he was in Oregon', and 'We expect him back in a few weeks'. I'm not saying this was necessarily better, let alone more character-forming; just that in my case it probably helped not to have my parents a button's touch away, spilling out anxieties and long-range weather forecasts, warning me against floods, epidemics and psychos who preyed on backpackers.

I met a girl while I was out there: Annie. She was American, travelling round like me. We hooked up, as she put it, and spent three months together. She wore plaid shirts, had grey-green eyes and a friendly manner; we became lovers easily and quickly; I couldn't believe my luck. Nor could I believe how simple it was: to be friends and bed-companions, to laugh and drink and smoke a little dope together, to see a bit of the world side by side – and then to separate without recrimination or blame. Easy come, easy go, she said, and meant it. Later, looking back, I wondered if something in me wasn't shocked by this very easiness, and didn't require more complication as proof of . . . what? Depth, seriousness? Although, God knows you can have complication and difficulty without any compensating depth or seriousness. Much later, I also found myself debating whether 'Easy come, easy go' wasn't a way of asking a question, and looking for a particular answer I wasn't able to supply. Still, that's all by the by. Annie was part of my story, but not of this story.

My parents thought of getting in touch when it happened, but had no idea where I was. In a true emergency – presence required at a mother's deathbed – I imagine the Foreign Office would have contacted the Embassy in Washington, who would have informed the American authorities, who would have asked police forces across the country to look out for a cheerful, sunburnt Englishman who was a little more self-assured than he had been on his arrival in the country. Nowadays all it takes is a text message.

When I got home, my mother gave me a stiff-armed, face-powdered hug, sent me off for a bath, and cooked me what was still referred to as my 'favourite dinner', and which I accepted as such, not having updated her for a while on my taste buds. Afterwards, she handed me the very few letters that had arrived in my absence.

'You'd better open those two first.'

The top one contained a brief note from Alex. 'Dear Tony,' it read, 'Adrian died. He killed himself. I rang your mother, who says she doesn't know where you are. Alex.'

'Shit,' I said, swearing for the first time in front of my parents.

'Sorry about that, lad.' My father's comment didn't seem exactly up to the mark. I looked at him and found myself wondering if baldness was inherited – would be inherited.

After one of those communal pauses which every family does differently, my mother asked, 'Do you think it was because he was too clever?'

'I haven't got the statistics linking intelligence to suicide,' I replied.

'Yes, Tony, but you know what I mean.'

'No, actually, I don't at all.'

'Well, put it like this: you're a clever boy, but not so clever as you'd do anything like that.'

I gazed at her without thinking. Wrongly encouraged, she went on,

'But if you're very clever, I think there's something that can unhinge you if you're not careful.'

To avoid engaging with this line of theory, I opened Alex's second letter. He said that Adrian had done it very efficiently, and left a full account of his reasons. 'Let's meet and talk. Bar at the Charing X Hotel? Phone me. Alex.'

I unpacked, readjusted, reported on my travels, familiarised myself again with the routines and smells, the small pleasures and large dullnesses of home. But my mind kept returning to all those fervently innocent discussions we'd gone in for when Robson hanged himself in the attic, back before our lives began. It had seemed to us philosophically self-evident that suicide was every free person's right: a logical act when faced with terminal illness or senility; a heroic one when faced with torture or the avoidable deaths of others; a glamorous one in the fury of disappointed love (see: Great Literature). None of these categories had applied in the case of Robson's squalidly mediocre action.

Nor did any of them apply to Adrian. In the letter he left for the coroner he had explained his reasoning: that life is a gift bestowed without anyone asking for it; that the thinking person has a philosophical duty to examine both the nature of life and the conditions it comes with; and that if this person decides to renounce the gift no one asks for, it is a moral and human duty to act on the consequences of that decision. There was practically a QED at the end. Adrian had asked the coroner to make his argument public, and the official had obliged.

Eventually, I asked, 'How did he do it?'

'He cut his wrists in the bath.'

'Christ. That's sort of . . . Greek, isn't it? Or was that hemlock?'

'More the exemplary Roman, I'd say. Opening the vein. And he knew how to do it. You have to cut diagonally. If you cut straight across, you can lose consciousness and the wound closes up and you've bogged it.'

'Perhaps you just drown instead.'

'Even so – second prize,' said Alex. 'Adrian would have wanted first.' He was right: first-class degree, first-class suicide.

He'd killed himself in a flat he shared with two fellow postgraduates. The others had gone away for the weekend, so Adrian had plenty of time to prepare. He'd written his letter to the coroner, pinned a notice to the bathroom door reading 'DO NOT ENTER – CALL POLICE – ADRIAN', run a bath, locked the door, cut his wrists in the hot water, bled to death. He was found a day and a half later.

Alex showed me a clipping from the *Cambridge Evening News*. 'Tragic Death of "Promising" Young Man'. They probably kept that headline permanently set up in type. The verdict of the coroner's inquest had been that Adrian Finn (22) had killed himself 'while the balance of his mind was disturbed'. I remember how angry that conventional phrase made me: I would have sworn on oath that Adrian's was the one mind which would never lose its balance. But in the law's view, if you killed yourself you were by definition mad, at least at the time you were committing the act. The law, and society, and religion all said it was impossible to be sane, healthy, and kill yourself. Perhaps those authorities feared that the suicide's reasoning might impugn the nature and value of life as organised by the state which paid the coroner? And then, since you had been declared temporarily mad, your reasons for killing yourself were also assumed to be mad. So I doubt anyone paid much attention to Adrian's argument, with its references to philosophers ancient and modern, about the superiority of the intervening act over the unworthy passivity of merely letting life happen to you.

Adrian had apologised to the police for inconveniencing them, and thanked the coroner for making his last words public. He also asked to be cremated, and for his ashes to be scattered, since the swift destruction of the body was also a philosopher's active choice, and preferable to the supine waiting for natural decomposition in the ground.

'Did you go? To the funeral?'

'Not invited. Nor was Colin. Family only, and all that.'

'What do we think?'

'Well, it's the family's right, I suppose.'

'No, not about that. About his reasons.'

Alex took a sip of his beer. 'I couldn't decide whether it's fucking impressive or a fucking terrible waste.'

'And did you? Decide?'

'Well, it could be both.'

'What I can't work out,' I said, 'is if it's something complete in itself – I don't mean self-regarding but, you know, just involving Adrian – or something that contains an implicit criticism of everyone else. Of us.' I looked at Alex.

'Well, it could be both.'

'Stop saying that.'

'I wonder what his philosophy tutors thought. Whether they felt in any way responsible. It was his brain they trained, after all.'

'When did you last see him?'

'About three months before he died. Right where you're sitting. That's why I suggested it.'

'So he was going down to Chislehurst. How did he seem?'

'Cheerful. Happy. Like himself, only more so. As we said goodbye, he told me he was in love.'

The bitch, I thought. If there was one woman in the entire world a man could fall in love with and still think life worth refusing, it was Veronica.

'What did he say about her?'

'Nothing. You know how he was.'

'Did he tell you I wrote him a letter telling him where to shove it?'

'No, but it doesn't surprise me.'

'What, that I wrote it, or that he didn't tell you?'

'Well, it could be both.'

I half-punched Alex, just enough to spill his beer.

At home, with barely enough time to think over what I'd heard, I had to fend off my mother's questions.

'What did you find out?'

I told her a little of the how.

'It must have been very unpleasant for the poor policemen. The things they have to do. Did he have girl trouble?'

Part of me wanted to say: Of course – he was going out with Veronica. Instead, I merely replied, 'Alex said he was happy the last time they met.'

'So why did he do it?'

I gave her the short version of the short version, leaving out the names of the relevant philosophers. I tried to explain about refusing an unsought gift, about action versus passivity. My mother nodded away as she took all this in.

'You see, I was right.'

'How's that, Ma?'

'He *was* too clever. If you're that clever you can argue yourself into anything. You just leave common sense behind. It's his brain unhinged him, that's why he did it.'

'Yes, Ma.'

'Is that all you've got to say? You mean you agree?'

Not replying was the only way to keep my temper.

I spent the next few days trying to think round all the angles and corners of Adrian's death. While I could hardly have expected a farewell letter myself, I was disappointed for Colin and Alex. And how was I to think about Veronica now? Adrian loved her, yet he had killed himself: how was that explicable? For most of us, the first experience of love, even if it doesn't work out – perhaps especially when it doesn't work out – promises that here is the thing that validates, that vindicates life. And though subsequent years might alter this view, until some of us give up on it altogether, when love first strikes, there's nothing like it, is there? Agreed?

But Adrian didn't agree. Perhaps if it had been a different woman . . . or perhaps not – Alex had testified to Adrian's exalted state the last time they'd met. Had something terrible happened in the intervening months? But if so, Adrian would surely have indicated it. He was the truth-seeker and philosopher among us: if those were his stated reasons, those were his true reasons.

With Veronica, I moved from blaming her for having failed to save Adrian to pitying her: there she was, having triumphantly traded up, and look what had happened. Should I express my condolences? But she would think me hypocritical. If I were to get in touch with her, either she wouldn't reply, or she'd somehow twist things so that I'd end up not being able to think straight.

I did, eventually, find myself thinking straight. That's to say, understanding Adrian's reasons, respecting them, and admiring him. He had a better mind and a more rigorous temperament than me; he thought logically, and then acted on the conclusion of logical thought. Whereas most of us, I suspect, do the opposite: we make an instinctive decision, then build up an infrastructure of reasoning to justify it. And call the result common sense. Did I think Adrian's action an implied criticism of the rest of us? No. Or at least, I'm sure he didn't intend it as such. Adrian might attract people, but he never behaved as if he wanted disciples; he believed in us all thinking for ourselves. Might he have 'enjoyed life', as most of us do, or try to, had he lived? Perhaps; or he might have suffered guilt and remorse at having failed to match his actions to his arguments.

And none of the above alters the fact that it was still, as Alex put it, a fucking terrible waste.

A year on, Colin and Alex suggested a reunion. On the anniversary of Adrian's death, the three of us met for drinks at the Charing Cross Hotel, then went for an Indian meal. We tried to invoke and celebrate our friend. We remembered him telling Old Joe Hunt he was out of a job, and instructing Phil Dixon about Eros and Thanatos. We were already turning our past into anecdote. We recalled cheering the announcement that Adrian had won a scholarship to Cambridge. We realised that though he had been to all our homes, none of us had been to his; and that we didn't know – had we ever asked? – what his father did. We toasted him in wine at the hotel bar and in beer at the end of dinner. Outside, we slapped one another around the shoulders and swore to repeat the commemoration annually. But our lives were already going in different directions, and the shared memory of Adrian was not enough to hold us together. Perhaps the lack of mystery about his death meant that his case was more easily closed. We would remember him all our lives, of course. But his death was exemplary rather than 'tragic' – as the Cambridge newspaper had routinely insisted – and so he retreated from us rather quickly, slotted into time and history.

By now I'd left home, and started work as a trainee in arts administration. Then I met Margaret; we married, and three years later Susie was born. We bought a small house with a large mortgage; I commuted up to London every day. My traineeship turned into a long career. Life went by. Some Englishman once said that marriage is a long dull meal with the pudding served first. I think that's far too cynical. I enjoyed my marriage, but was perhaps too quiet – too peaceable – for my own good. After a dozen years Margaret took up with a fellow who ran a restaurant. I didn't much like him – or his food, for that matter – but then I wouldn't, would I? Custody of Susie was shared. Happily, she didn't seem too affected by the break-up; and, as I now realise, I never applied to her my theory of damage.

After the divorce, I had a few affairs, but nothing serious. I would always tell Margaret about any new girlfriend. At the time, it seemed a natural thing to do. Now, I sometimes wonder if it was an attempt to make her jealous; or, perhaps, an act of self-protection, a way of preventing the new relationship from becoming too serious. Also, in my more emptied life, I came up with various ideas which I termed 'projects', perhaps to make them sound feasible. None of them came to anything. Well, that's no matter; or any part of my story.

Susie grew up, and people started calling her Susan. When she was twenty-four, I walked her up the aisle of a register office. Ken is a doctor; they have two kids now, a boy and a girl. The photos of them I carry in my wallet always show them younger than they are. That's normal, I suppose, not to say 'philosophically self-evident'. But you find yourself repeating, 'They grow up so quickly, don't they?' when all you really mean is: time goes faster for me nowadays.

Margaret's second husband turned out to be not quite peaceable enough: he took off with someone who looked rather like her, but was that crucial ten years younger. She and I remain on good terms; we meet at family events and sometimes have lunch. Once, after a glass or two, she became sentimental and suggested we might get back together. Odder things have happened, was the way she put it. No doubt they have, but by now I was used to my own routines, and fond of my solitude. Or maybe I'm just not odd enough to do something like that. Once or twice we've talked of sharing a holiday, but I think we each expected the other to plan it and book the tickets and hotels. So that never happened.

I'm retired now. I have my flat with my possessions. I keep up with a few drinking pals, and have some women friends – platonic, of course. (And they're not part of the story either.) I'm a member of the local history society, though less excited than some about what metal detectors unearth. A while ago, I volunteered to run the library at the local hospital; I go round the wards delivering, collecting, recommending. It gets me out, and it's good to do something useful; also, I meet some new people. Sick people, of course; dying people as well. But at least I shall know my way around the hospital when my turn comes.

And that's a life, isn't it? Some achievements and some disappointments. It's been interesting to me, though I wouldn't complain or be amazed if others found it less so. Maybe, in a way, Adrian knew what he was doing. Not that I would have missed my own life for anything, you understand.

I survived. 'He survived to tell the tale' – that's what people say, don't they? History isn't the lies of the victors, as I once glibly assured Old Joe Hunt; I know that now. It's more the memories of the survivors, most of whom are neither victorious nor defeated.

TWO

Later on in life, you expect a bit of rest, don't you? You think you deserve it. I did, anyway. But then you begin to understand that the reward of merit is not life's business.

Also, when you are young, you think you can predict the likely pains and bleaknesses that age might bring. You imagine yourself being lonely, divorced, widowed; children growing away from you, friends dying. You imagine the loss of status, the loss of desire – and desirability. You may go further and consider your own approaching death, which, despite what company you may muster, can only be faced alone. But all this is looking ahead. What you fail to do is look ahead, and then imagine yourself looking back from that future point. Learning the new emotions that time brings. Discovering, for example, that as the witnesses to your life diminish, there is less corroboration, and therefore less certainty, as to what you are or have been. Even if you have assiduously kept records – in words, sound, pictures – you may find that you have attended to the wrong kind of record-keeping. What was the line Adrian used to quote? 'History is that certainty produced at the point where the imperfections of memory meet the inadequacies of documentation.'

I still read a lot of history, and of course I've followed all the official history that's happened in my own lifetime – the

fall of Communism, Mrs Thatcher, 9/11, global warming –
with the normal mixture of fear, anxiety and cautious
optimism. But I've never felt the same about it – I've never
quite trusted it – as I do events in Greece and Rome, or
the British Empire, or the Russian Revolution. Perhaps I
just feel safer with the history that's been more or less
agreed upon. Or perhaps it's that same paradox again: the
history that happens underneath our noses ought to be the
clearest, and yet it's the most deliquescent. We live in time,
it bounds us and defines us, and time is supposed to measure
history, isn't it? But if we can't understand time, can't grasp
its mysteries of pace and progress, what chance do we have
with history – even our own small, personal, largely
undocumented piece of it?

When we're young, everyone over the age of thirty looks
middle-aged, everyone over fifty antique. And time, as it
goes by, confirms that we weren't that wrong. Those little
age differentials, so crucial and so gross when we are
young, erode. We end up all belonging to the same
category, that of the non-young. I've never much minded
this myself.

But there are exceptions to the rule. For some people,
the time differentials established in youth never really
disappear: the elder remains the elder, even when both are
dribbling greybeards. For some people, a gap of, say, five
months means that one will perversely always think of
himself – herself – as wiser and more knowledgeable than
the other, whatever the evidence to the contrary. Or perhaps
I should say *because* of the evidence to the contrary. *Because*
it is perfectly clear to any objective observer that the balance

has shifted to the marginally younger person, the other one maintains the assumption of superiority all the more rigorously. All the more neurotically.

I still play a lot of Dvořák, by the way. Not the symphonies so much; nowadays I prefer the string quartets. But Tchaikovsky has gone the way of those geniuses who fascinate in youth, retain a residual power in middle age, but later seem, if not embarrassing, somehow less relevant. Not that I'm saying she was right. There's nothing wrong with being a genius who can fascinate the young. Rather, there's something wrong with the young who can't be fascinated by a genius. Incidentally, I don't think the sound-track to *Un Homme et Une Femme* is a work of genius. I didn't even think so back then. On the other hand, I occasionally remember Ted Hughes and smile at the fact that, actually, he never did run out of animals.

I get on well with Susie. Well enough, anyway. But the younger generation no longer feels the need, or even the obligation, to keep in touch. At least, not 'keep in touch' as in 'seeing'. An email will do for Dad – pity he hasn't learnt to text. Yes, he's retired now, still fossicking around with those mysterious 'projects' of his, doubt he'll ever finish anything, but at least it keeps the brain active, better than golf, and yes, we were planning to drop over there last week until something came up. I do hope he doesn't get Alzheimer's, that's my greatest worry really, because, well, Mum's hardly going to have him back, is she? No: I exaggerate, I misrepresent. Susie doesn't feel like that, I'm sure. Living alone has its moments of self-pity and paranoia. Susie and I get on fine.

A friend of ours – I still say that instinctively, though Margaret and I have been divorced for longer than we were married – had a son in a punk rock band. I asked if she'd heard any of their songs. She mentioned one called 'Every Day is Sunday'. I remember laughing with relief that the same old adolescent boredom goes on from generation to generation. Also that the same sardonic wit is used to escape from it. 'Every day is Sunday' – the words took me back to my own years of stagnancy, and that terrible waiting for life to begin. I asked our friend what the group's other songs were. No, she replied, that's their song, their only song. How does it go then? I asked. What do you mean? Well, what's the next line? You don't get it, do you? she said. That *is* the song. They just repeat the line, again and again, until the song chooses to end. I remember smiling. 'Every day is Sunday' – that wouldn't make a bad epitaph, would it?

It was one of those long white envelopes with my name and address shown in a window. I don't know about you, but I'm never in a hurry to open them. Once, such letters meant another painful stage in my divorce – maybe that's why I'm wary of them. Nowadays, they might contain some tax voucher for the few, pitifully low-yielding shares I bought when I retired, or an extra request from that charity I already support by standing order. So I forgot about it until later in the day, when I was gathering up all the discarded paper in the flat – even down to the last envelope – for recycling. It turned out to contain a letter from a firm of solicitors I'd never heard of, Messrs Coyle, Innes & Black. A certain Eleanor Marriott was writing '<u>In the matter of the estate of Mrs Sarah Ford (deceased)</u>'. It took me a while to get there.

We live with such easy assumptions, don't we? For instance, that memory equals events plus time. But it's all much odder than this. Who was it said that memory is what we thought we'd forgotten? And it ought to be obvious to us that time doesn't act as a fixative, rather as a solvent. But it's not convenient – it's not useful – to believe this; it doesn't help us get on with our lives; so we ignore it.

I was asked to confirm my address and provide a photocopy of my passport. I was informed that I had been left five hundred pounds and two 'documents'. I found this very puzzling. For a start, to get a bequest from someone whose Christian name I had either never known or else forgotten. And five hundred pounds seemed a very specific sum. Bigger than nothing, not as big as something. Perhaps it would make sense if I knew when Mrs Ford had made her will. Though if it had been a long time ago, the equivalent sum now would be quite a bit larger, and make even less sense.

I confirmed my existence, authenticity and location, attaching photocopied corroboration. I asked if I might be told the date of the will. Then, one evening I sat down and tried to resurrect that humiliating weekend in Chislehurst some forty years previously. I searched for any moment, incident or remark which might have seemed worthy of acknowledgement or reward. But my memory has increasingly become a mechanism which reiterates apparently truthful data with little variation. I stared into the past, I waited, I tried to trick my memory into a different course. But it was no good. I was someone who had gone out with the daughter of Mrs Sarah Ford (deceased) for a period of about a year, who had been patronised by her husband, loftily scrutinised by her son, and manipulated by her daughter. Painful for me at the time, but hardly requiring the subsequent maternal apology of five hundred pounds.

And anyway, that pain hasn't lasted. As I mentioned, I have a certain instinct for self-preservation. I successfully put Veronica out of my mind, out of my history. So when time delivered me all too quickly into middle age, and I began looking back over how my life had unfolded, and considering the paths untaken, those lulling, undermining what-ifs, I never found myself imagining – not even for worse, let alone for better – how things would have been with Veronica. Annie yes, Veronica no. And I never regretted my years with Margaret, even if we did divorce. Try as I could – which wasn't very hard – I rarely ended up fantasising a markedly different life from the one that has been mine. I don't think this is complacency; it's more likely a lack of imagination, or ambition, or something. I suppose the truth is that, yes, I'm not odd enough not to have done the things I've ended up doing with my life.

★

I didn't read the solicitor's letter immediately. Instead, I looked at the enclosure, a long, creamy envelope with my name on it. Handwriting I had seen only once in my life before, but nonetheless familiar. Anthony Webster Esq. – the way the ascenders and descenders finished with a little curlicue took me back to someone I had known for a mere weekend. Someone whose handwriting, in its confidence rather than shape, suggested a woman perhaps 'odd enough' to do things I hadn't. But what they might have been, I couldn't know or guess. There was an inch of Sellotape on the front of the envelope, centre top. I was expecting it to run down the back and add an extra seal, but it had been cut off along the envelope's top edge. Presumably the letter had once been attached to something else.

Finally, I opened it and read. 'Dear Tony, I think it right you should have the attached. Adrian always spoke warmly of you, and perhaps you will find it an interesting, if painful, memento of long ago. I am also leaving you a little money. You may find this strange, and to tell the truth I am not quite sure of my own motives. In any case, I am sorry for the way my family treated you all those years ago, and wish you well, even from beyond the grave. Yours, Sarah Ford. P.S. It may sound odd, but I think the last months of his life were happy.'

The solicitor asked for my bank details so that the legacy could be paid direct. She added that she was enclosing the first of the 'documents' I had been left. The second was still in the possession of Mrs Ford's daughter. That, I realised, would explain the cut piece of Sellotape. Mrs Marriott was currently trying to obtain this second item. And Mrs Ford's will, in answer to my question, had been drawn up five years previously.

★

Margaret used to say that there were two sorts of women: those with clear edges to them, and those who implied mystery. And that this was the first thing a man sensed, and the first thing that attracted him, or not. Some men are drawn to one type, some to the other. Margaret – you won't need me to tell you – was clear-edged, but at times she could be envious of those who carried, or manufactured, an air of mystery.

'I like you just as you are,' I once said to her.

'But you know me so well by now,' she replied. We had been married about six or seven years. 'Wouldn't you prefer it if I were a little more . . . unknowable?'

'I don't want you to be a woman of mystery. I think I'd hate it. Either it's just a façade, a game, a technique for ensnaring men, or else the woman of mystery is a mystery even to herself, and that's the worst of all.'

'Tony, you sound like a real man of the world.'

'Well, I'm not,' I said – aware, of course, that she was teasing me. 'I haven't known that many women in my life.'

'"I may not know much about women, but I know what I like"?'

'I didn't say that, and I don't mean it either. But I think it's because I've known comparatively few that I know what I think about them. And what I like about them. If I'd known more, I'd be more confused.'

Margaret said, 'Now I'm not sure whether to be flattered or not.'

All this was before our marriage went wrong, of course. But it wouldn't have lasted any longer if Margaret had been more mysterious, I can assure you – and her – of that.

*

And something of her rubbed off on me over the years. For instance, if I hadn't known her, I might have become involved in a patient exchange of letters with the solicitor. But I didn't want to wait quietly for another envelope with a window. Instead, I rang up Mrs Eleanor Marriott and asked about the other document I'd been left.

'The will describes it as a diary.'

'A diary? Is it Mrs Ford's?'

'No. Let me check the name.' A pause. 'Adrian Finn.'

Adrian! How had Mrs Ford ended up with his diary? Which was not a question for the solicitor. 'He was a friend,' was all I said. Then, 'Presumably it was attached to the letter you sent.'

'I can't be sure of that.'

'Have you actually seen it?'

'No, I haven't.' Her manner was properly cautious, rather than unhelpful.

'Did Veronica Ford give any reason for withholding it?'

'She said she wasn't ready to part with it yet.'

Right. 'But it is mine?'

'It was certainly left to you in the will.'

Hmm. I wondered if there was some legal nicety separating those two propositions. 'Do you know how she . . . came by it?'

'She was living not far from her mother in the last years, as I understand it. She said she took various items into her safekeeping. In case the house was burgled. Jewellery, money, documents.'

'Is that legal?'

'Well, it's not illegal. It may well be prudent.'

We didn't seem to be getting very far. 'Let me get this straight. She ought to have handed over this document, this diary, to you. You've asked for it, and she's refusing to give it up.'

'For the present, yes, that is the case.'

'Can you give me her address?'

'I would have to have her authority to do so.'

'Then would you kindly seek that authority?'

Have you noticed how, when you talk to someone like a solicitor, after a while you stop sounding like yourself and end up sounding like them?

The less time there remains in your life, the less you want to waste it. That's logical, isn't it? Though how you use the saved-up hours . . . well, that's another thing you probably wouldn't have predicted in youth. For instance, I spend a lot of time clearing things up – and I'm not even a messy person. But it's one of the modest satisfactions of age. I aim for tidiness; I recycle; I clean and decorate my flat to keep up its value. I've made my will; and my dealings with my daughter, son-in-law, grandchildren and ex-wife are, if less than perfect, at least settled. Or so I've persuaded myself. I've achieved a state of peaceableness, even peacefulness. Because I get on with things. I don't like mess, and I don't like leaving a mess. I've opted for cremation, if you want to know.

So I phoned Mrs Marriott again, and asked for the contact details of Mrs Ford's other child, John, known as Jack. I called Margaret and asked for a lunch date. And I made an appointment with my own solicitor. No, that's putting it far too grandly. I'm sure Brother Jack would have someone he refers to as 'my solicitor'. In my case it's the local chap who drew up my will; he has a small office above a florist's and seems perfectly efficient. I also like him because he made no attempt to use my Christian name or suggest I use his. So I think of him only as T. J. Gunnell, and don't even speculate on what his initials might stand for. Do you know something I dread? Being an old person in hospital and having nurses I've never met calling me Anthony or, worse, Tony. Let me just pop this in your arm, Tony. Have some more of this gruel, Tony. Have you done a motion, Tony? Of course, by the time this happens, over-familiarity from the nursing staff may be way down my list of anxieties; but even so.

I did a slightly odd thing when I first met Margaret. I wrote Veronica out of my life story. I pretended that Annie had been my first proper girlfriend. I know most men exaggerate the amount of girls and sex they've had; I did the opposite. I drew a line and started afresh. Margaret was a little puzzled that I'd been so slow off the mark – not in losing my virginity, but in having a serious relationship; but also, I thought at the time, a little charmed. She said something about shyness being attractive in a man.

The odder part was that it was easy to give this version of my history because that's what I'd been telling myself anyway. I viewed my time with Veronica as a failure – her contempt, my humiliation – and expunged it from the record. I had kept no letters, and only a single photograph, which I hadn't looked at in ages.

But after a year or two of marriage, when I felt better about myself, and fully confident in our relationship, I told Margaret the truth. She listened, asked pertinent questions, and she understood. She asked to see the photo – the one taken in Trafalgar Square – examined it, nodded, made no comment. That was fine. I had no right to expect anything, let alone words of praise for my former girlfriend. Which, in any case, I didn't want. I just wanted to clear off the past, and have Margaret forgive my peculiar lie about it. Which she did.

Mr Gunnell is a calm, gaunt man who doesn't mind silence. After all, it costs his clients just as much as speech.

'Mr Webster.'

'Mr Gunnell.'

And so we mistered one another for the next forty-five minutes, in which he gave me the professional advice I was paying for. He told me that going to the police and trying to persuade them to lay a charge of theft against a woman of mature years who had recently lost her mother would, in his view, be foolish. I liked that. Not the advice, but the way he expressed it. 'Foolish': much better than 'inadvisable' or 'inappropriate'. He also urged me not to badger Mrs Marriott.

'Don't solicitors like to be badgered, Mr Gunnell?'

'Let's say it's different if the badgerer is the client. But in the present case the Ford family is paying the bills. And you'd be surprised how letters can slip to the bottom of a file.'

I looked around the cream-painted office with its potted plants, shelves of legal authority, inoffensive print of an English landscape and, yes, its filing cabinets. I looked back to Mr Gunnell.

'In other words, don't let her start thinking I'm some kind of loony.'

'Oh, she'd never think that, Mr Webster. And "loony" is hardly legal terminology.'

'What might you say instead?'

'We might settle for "vexatious". That's quite strong enough.'

'Right. And on another point. How long does it take to wind up an estate?'

'If it's fairly straightforward . . . eighteen months, two years.'

Two years! I wasn't waiting that long for the diary.

'Well, you deal with the main business first, but there are always things that drag on. Lost share certificates. Agreeing figures with the Revenue. And letters sometimes get mislaid.'

'Or slip to the bottom of a file.'

'That too, Mr Webster.'

'Have you any other advice?'

'I'd be careful with the word "stealing". It might polarise matters unnecessarily.'

'But isn't that what she's done? Remind me of the legal tag when something is blindingly obvious.'

'*Res ipsa loquitur*?'

'That's the one.'

Mr Gunnell paused. 'Well, criminal work doesn't often cross my desk, but the key phrase when it comes to theft is, as I remember, "an intention permanently to deprive" the owner of the thing stolen. Do you have any clue as to Miss Ford's intention, or her wider state of mind?'

I laughed. Having a clue as to Veronica's state of mind had been one of my problems forty years ago. So I probably laughed in quite the wrong way; and Mr Gunnell is not an imperceptive man.

'I don't wish to pry, Mr Webster, but could there be something in the past, perhaps, between you and Miss Ford, which might become relevant, were it eventually to come to civil or indeed criminal proceedings?'

Something between me and Miss Ford? A particular image suddenly came into my mind as I gazed at the backs of what I assumed to be family photographs.

'You've made things much clearer, Mr Gunnell. I'll put a first-class stamp on when I pay your bill.'

He smiled. 'Actually, it's a thing we do notice. In certain cases.'

Mrs Marriott was able, two weeks later, to provide me with an email address for Mr John Ford. Miss Veronica Ford had declined to allow her contact details to be passed on. And Mr John Ford was clearly being cautious himself: no phone number, no postal address.

I remembered Brother Jack sitting back on a sofa, careless and confident. Veronica had just ruffled my hair and was asking, 'He'll do, won't he?' And Jack had winked at me. I hadn't winked back.

I was formal in my email. I offered my condolences. I pretended to happier memories of Chislehurst than was the case. I explained the situation and asked Jack to use what influence he had to persuade his sister to hand over the second 'document', which I understood to be the diary of my old schoolfriend Adrian Finn.

About ten days later Brother Jack turned up in my inbox. There was a long preamble about travelling, and semi-retirement, and the humidity of Singapore, and Wi-Fi and cybercafés. And then: 'Anyway, enough chit-chat. Regret

I am not my sister's keeper – never have been, just between ourselves. Stopped trying to change her mind years ago. And frankly, my putting in a good word for you could easily have the opposite effect. Not that I don't wish you well on this particular sticky wicket. Ah – here comes my rickshaw – must dash. Regards, John Ford.'

Why did I feel there was something unconvincing about all this? Why did I immediately picture him sitting quietly at home – in some plush mansion backing on to a golf course in Surrey – laughing at me? His server was aol.com, which didn't tell me anything. I looked at his email's timing, which was plausible for both Singapore and Surrey. Why did I imagine Brother Jack had seen me coming and was having a bit of fun? Perhaps because in this country shadings of class resist time longer than differentials in age. The Fords had been posher than the Websters back then, and they were jolly well going to stay that way. Or was this mere paranoia on my part?

Nothing to be done, of course, but email back politely and ask if he could let me have Veronica's contact details.

When people say, 'She's a good-looking woman,' they usually mean, 'She used to be a good-looking woman.' But when I say that about Margaret, I mean it. She thinks – she knows – that she's changed, and she has; though less to me than to anybody else. Naturally, I can't speak for the restaurant manager. But I'd put it like this: she sees only what's gone, I see only what's stayed the same. Her hair is no longer halfway down her back or pulled up in a French pleat; nowadays it is cut close to her skull and the grey is allowed to show. Those peasanty frocks she used to wear have given way to cardigans and well-cut trousers. Some of the freckles I once loved are now closer to liver spots. But it's still the eyes we look at, isn't it? That's where we found the other person, and find them still. The same eyes that were in the same head when we first met, slept together, married, honeymooned, joint-mortgaged, shopped, cooked and holidayed, loved one another and had a child together. And were the same when we separated.

But it's not just the eyes. The bone structure stays the same, as do the instinctive gestures, the many ways of being herself. And her way, even after all this time and distance, of being with me.

'So what's all this about, Tony?'

I laughed. We had barely looked at our menus, but I didn't find the question premature. That's what Margaret's like. When you say you're not sure about a second child, do you mean you're not sure about having one with me? Why do you think divorce is about apportioning blame? What are you going to do with the rest of your life now? If you'd really wanted to go on holiday with me, wouldn't it have helped to book some tickets? And what's all this about, Tony?

Some people are insecure about their partners' previous lovers, as if they fear them still. Margaret and I were exempt from that. Not that in my case there was exactly a crocodile of ex-girlfriends all lined up. And if she allowed herself to give them nicknames, that was her right, wasn't it?

'Actually, of all people, it's about Veronica Ford.'

'The Fruitcake?' I knew she'd say that, so I didn't wince. 'Is she back in business after all these years? You were well out of *that*, Tony.'

'I know,' I replied. It's possible that when I finally got

around to telling Margaret about Veronica, I'd laid it on a bit, made myself sound more of a dupe, and Veronica more unstable than she'd been. But since it was my account that had given rise to the nickname, I couldn't very well object to it. All I could do was not use it myself.

I told her the story, what I'd done, how I'd approached things. As I say, something of Margaret had rubbed off on me over the years, which is perhaps why she nodded in agreement or encouragement at various points.

'Why do you think the Fruitcake's mother left you five hundred pounds?'

'I haven't the slightest idea.'

'And you think the brother was stringing you along?'

'Yes. Or at least, not being natural with me.'

'But you don't know him at all, do you?'

'I only met him once, it's true. I guess I'm just suspicious of the whole family.'

'And why do you think the mother ended up with the diary?'

'I've no idea.'

'Perhaps Adrian left it to her because he didn't trust the Fruitcake.'

'That doesn't make sense.'

There was a silence. We ate. Then Margaret tapped her knife against my plate.

'And if the presumably still-unmarried Miss Veronica Ford happened to walk into this café and sit down at our table, how would the long-divorced Mr Anthony Webster react?'

She always puts her finger on it, doesn't she?

'I don't think I'd be especially pleased to see her.'

Something in the formality of my tone caused Margaret

to smile. 'Intrigued? Start rolling up your sleeve and taking off your watch?'

I blushed. You haven't seen a bald man in his sixties blush? Oh, it happens, just as it does to a hairy, spotty fifteen-year-old. And because it's rarer, it sends the blusher tumbling back to that time when life felt like nothing more than one long sequence of embarrassments.

'I wish I hadn't told you that.'

She took a forkful of rocket and tomato salad.

'Sure there isn't some . . . undoused fire in your breast, Mr Webster?'

'I'm pretty positive.'

'Well then, unless she gets in touch with you, I'd leave it. Cash the cheque, take me on a budget holiday, and forget it. Two fifty each might get us all the way to the Channel Islands.'

'I like it when you tease me,' I said. 'Even after all these years.'

She leant across and patted my hand. 'It's nice that we're still fond of one another. And it's nice that I know you'll never get around to booking that holiday.'

'Only because I know you don't mean it.'

She smiled. And for a moment, she almost looked enigmatic. But Margaret can't do enigma, that first step to Woman of Mystery. If she'd wanted me to spend the money on a holiday for two, she'd have said so. Yes, I realise that's exactly what she *did* say, but . . .

But anyway. 'She's stolen my stuff,' I said, perhaps a little whinily.

'How do you know you want it?'

'It's Adrian's diary. He's my friend. He was my friend. It's mine.'

'If your friend had wanted you to have his diary, he could have left it to you forty years ago, and cut out the middleman. Or woman.'

'Yes.'

'What do you think's in it?'

'I've no idea. It's just mine.' I recognised at that moment another reason for my determination. The diary was evidence; it was – it might be – corroboration. It might disrupt the banal reiterations of memory. It might jump-start something – though I had no idea what.

'Well, you can always find out where the Fruitcake lives. Friends Reunited, telephone directory, private detective. Go round, ring the doorbell, ask for your stuff.'

'No.'

'Which leaves burglary,' she suggested cheerily.

'You're joking.'

'Then let it go. Unless you have, as they say, issues from your past that you need to confront in order to be able to move on. But that's hardly you, is it, Tony?'

'No, I don't think so,' I answered, rather carefully. Because part of me was wondering if, psychobabble apart, there might not be some truth in it. There was a silence. Our plates were cleared. Margaret didn't have any problem reading me.

'It's quite touching that you're so stubborn. I suppose it's one way of not losing the plot when we get to our age.'

'I don't think I'd have reacted differently twenty years ago.'

'Possibly not.' She made a sign for the bill. 'But let me tell you a story about Caroline. No, you don't know her. She's a friend from after we separated. She had a husband, two small kids and an au pair she wasn't sure about. She didn't have any dreadful suspicions or anything. The girl was polite most of the time, the children didn't complain. It was just that Caroline felt she didn't really know who she was leaving them with. So she asked a friend – a female friend – no, not me – if she had any advice. "Go through her stuff," said the friend. "What?" "Well, you're obviously wound up about it. Wait till it's her evening off, have a look through her room, read her letters. That's what I'd do." So the next time the au pair was off, Caroline went through her stuff. And found the girl's diary. Which she read. And which was full of denunciations, like "I'm working for a real cow" and "The husband's OK – caught him looking at my bum – but the wife's a silly bitch." And "Does she know what she's doing to those poor kids?" There was some really, *really* tough stuff.'

'So what happened?' I asked. 'Did she fire the au pair?'

'Tony,' my ex-wife replied, 'that's not the point of the story.'

I nodded. Margaret checked the bill, running the corner of her credit card down the items.

Two other things she said over the years: that there were some women who aren't at all mysterious, but are only made so by men's inability to understand them. And that, in her view, fruitcakes ought to be shut up in tins with the Queen's head on them. I must have told her that detail of my Bristol life as well.

A week or so passed, and Brother Jack's name was there in my inbox again. 'Here's Veronica's email, but don't let on you got it from me. Hell to pay and all that. Remember the 3 wise monkeys – see no evil, hear no evil, speak no evil. That's my motto, anyway. Blue skies, view of Sydney Harbour Bridge, almost. Ah, here comes my rickshaw. Regards, John F.'

I was surprised. I'd expected him to be unhelpful. But what did I know of him or his life? Only what I'd extrapolated from memories of a bad weekend long before. I'd always assumed that birth and education had given him an advantage over me that he'd effortlessly maintained until the present day. I remembered Adrian saying that he'd read about Jack in some undergraduate magazine but didn't expect to meet him (but nor had he expected to go out with Veronica). And then he'd added, in a different, harsher tone, 'I *hate* the way the English have of not being serious about being serious.' I never knew – because stupidly I never asked – what that had been based on.

They say time finds you out, don't they? Maybe time had found out Brother Jack and punished him for his lack of seriousness. And now I began to elaborate a different life for Veronica's brother, one in which his student years glowed in his memory as filled with happiness and hope – indeed, as the one period when his life had briefly achieved that sense of harmony we all aspire to. I imagined Jack, after graduation, being nepotistically placed into one of those large multinational companies. I imagined him doing well enough to begin with and then, almost imperceptibly, not so well. A clubbable fellow with decent manners, but lacking the edge required in a changing world. Those cheery sign-offs, in letter and conversation, came after a while to appear not sophisticated but inept. And though he wasn't exactly given the push, the suggestion of early retirement combined with occasional bits of ad hoc work was clear enough. He could be a kind of roving honorary consul, a backup for the local man in big cities, a troubleshooter in smaller ones. So he remade his life, and found some plausible way to present himself as a success. 'View of Sydney Harbour Bridge, almost.' I imagined him taking his laptop to café terraces with Wi-Fi, because frankly that felt less depressing than working from the room of a hotel with fewer stars than he'd been previously used to.

I've no idea if this is how big firms work, but I'd found a way of thinking about Brother Jack which brought no discomfort. I'd even managed to dislodge him from that mansion overlooking the golf course. Not that I would go so far as to feel sorry for him. And – this was the point – not that I owed him anything either.

'Dear Veronica,' I began. 'Your brother has very kindly given me your email address . . .'

It strikes me that this may be one of the differences between youth and age: when we are young, we invent different futures for ourselves; when we are old, we invent different pasts for others.

Her father drove a Humber Super Snipe. Cars don't have names like that any more, do they? I drive a Volkswagen Polo. But Humber Super Snipe – those were words that eased off the tongue as smoothly as 'the Father, the Son and the Holy Ghost'. Humber Super Snipe. Armstrong Siddeley Sapphire. Jowett Javelin. Jensen Interceptor. Even Wolseley Farina and Hillman Minx.

Don't get me wrong. I'm not interested in cars, old or new. I'm vaguely curious why you might name a large saloon after such a small game bird as the snipe, and whether a Minx had a tempestuous female nature. Still, I'm not curious enough to find out. At this stage I prefer not to know.

But I've been turning over in my mind the question of nostalgia, and whether I suffer from it. I certainly don't get soggy at the memory of some childhood knick-knack; nor do I want to deceive myself sentimentally about something that wasn't even true at the time – love of the old school, and so on. But if nostalgia means the powerful recollection of strong emotions – and a regret that such feelings are no longer present in our lives – then I plead guilty. I'm nostalgic for my early time with Margaret, for Susie's birth and first years, for that road trip with Annie. And if we're talking about strong feelings that will never come again, I suppose it's possible to be nostalgic about remembered pain as well as remembered pleasure. And that opens up the field, doesn't it? It also leads straight to the matter of Miss Veronica Ford.

'Blood money?'

I looked at the words and couldn't make sense of them. She'd erased my message and its heading, not signed her reply, and just answered with a phrase. I had to call up my sent email and read it through again to work out that grammatically her two words could only be a reply to my asking why her mother had left me five hundred pounds. But it didn't make any sense beyond this. No blood had been spilt. My pride had been hurt, that was true. But

Veronica was hardly suggesting that her mother was offering money in exchange for the pain her daughter had caused me, was she? Or was she?

At the same time, it made sense that Veronica didn't give me a simple answer, didn't do or say what I hoped or expected. In this she was at least consistent with my memory of her. Of course, at times I'd been tempted to set her down as the woman of mystery, as opposed to the woman of clarity I married in Margaret. True, I hadn't known where I was with her, couldn't read her heart or her mind or her motivation. But an enigma is a puzzle you want to solve. I didn't want to solve Veronica, certainly not at this late date. She'd been a bloody difficult young woman forty years ago, and – on the evidence of this two-word, two-finger response – didn't seem to have mellowed with age. That's what I told myself firmly.

Though why should we expect age to mellow us? If it isn't life's business to reward merit, why should it be life's business to give us warm, comfortable feelings towards its end? What possible evolutionary purpose could nostalgia serve?

I had a friend who trained as a lawyer, then became disenchanted and never practised. He told me that the one benefit of those wasted years was that he no longer feared either the law or lawyers. And something like that happens more generally, doesn't it? The more you learn, the less you fear. 'Learn' not in the sense of academic study, but in the practical understanding of life.

Perhaps all I'm really saying is that, having gone out with Veronica all those years ago, I wasn't afraid of her now. And so I began my email campaign. I was determined to be polite, unoffendable, persistent, boring, friendly: in other words, to lie. Of course, it only takes a microsecond to delete an email, but then it doesn't take much longer to replace the one deleted. I would wear her down with niceness, and I would get Adrian's diary. There was no 'undoused fire in my breast' – I had assured Margaret of this. And as for her more general advice, let's say that one advantage of being an ex-husband is that you no longer need to justify your behaviour. Or follow suggestions.

I could tell Veronica was perplexed by my approach. Sometimes she answered briefly and crossly, often not at all. Nor would she have been flattered to know the precedent for my plan. Towards the end of my marriage, the solid suburban villa Margaret and I lived in suffered a little subsidence. Cracks appeared here and there, bits of the porch and front wall began to crumble. (And no, I didn't think of it as symbolic.) The insurance company ignored the fact that it had been a famously dry summer, and decided to blame the lime tree in our front garden. It wasn't an especially beautiful tree, nor was I fond of it, for various reasons: it screened out light from the front room, dropped sticky stuff on the pavement, and overhung the street in a way that encouraged pigeons to perch there and crap on the cars parked beneath. Our car, especially.

My objection to cutting it down was based on principle: not the principle of maintaining the country's stock of trees, but the principle of not kowtowing to unseen bureaucrats, baby-faced arborists, and current faddy theories of blame adduced by insurance companies. Also, Margaret quite liked the tree. So I prepared a long defensive campaign. I queried the arborist's conclusions and requested the digging of extra inspection pits to confirm or disprove the presence of rootlets close to the house's foundations; I argued over weather patterns, the great London clay-belt, the imposition of a region-wide hosepipe ban, and so on. I was rigidly polite; I aped my opponents' bureaucratic language; I annoyingly attached copies of previous correspondence to each new letter; I invited further site inspections and suggested extra use for their manpower. With each letter, I managed to come up with another query they would have to spend their time considering; if they failed to answer it, my next letter, instead of repeating the query, would refer them to the third or fourth paragraph of my communication of the 17th inst, so that they would have to look up their ever-fattening file. I was careful not to come across as a loony, but rather as a pedantic, unignorable bore. I liked to imagine the moaning and groaning as yet another of my letters arrived; and I knew that at a certain point it would make bean-counting sense for them to just close the case. Eventually, exasperatedly, they proposed a thirty per cent reduction in the lime tree's canopy, a solution I accepted with deep expressions of regret and much inner exhilaration.

Veronica, as I'd anticipated, didn't enjoy being treated like an insurance company. I'll spare you the tedium of our exchanges and cut to its first practical consequence. I received a letter from Mrs Marriott enclosing what she described as 'a fragment of the disputed document'. She expressed the hope that the next months might bring a full restitution of my legacy. I thought this showed a lot of optimism.

The 'fragment' turned out to be a photocopy of a fragment. But – even after forty years – I knew it was authentic. Adrian wrote in a distinctive italic hand with an eccentric 'g'. Needless to say, Veronica hadn't sent me the first page, or the last, or indicated where this one came in the diary. If 'diary' was still the right word for a text set out in numbered paragraphs. This is what I read:

5.4 The question of accumulation. If life is a wager, what form does the bet take? At the racetrack, an accumulator is a bet which rolls on profits from the success of one horse to engross the stake on the next one.
5.5 So a) To what extent might human relationships be expressed in a mathematical or logical formula? And b) If so, what signs might be placed between the integers? Plus and minus, self-evidently; sometimes multiplication, and yes, division. But these signs are limited. Thus an entirely failed relationship might be expressed in terms of both loss/minus and division/reduction, showing a total of zero; whereas an entirely successful one can be represented by both addition and multiplication. But what of most relationships? Do they not require to be expressed in notations which are logically improbable and mathematically insoluble?
5.6 Thus how might you express an accumulation containing the integers b, a^1, a^2, s, v?

$$b = s - v \frac{\times}{+} a^1$$
or $a^2 + v + a^1 \times s = b$?

5.7 Or is that the wrong way to put the question and express the accumulation? Is the application of logic to the human condition in and of itself self-defeating? What becomes of a chain of argument when the links are made of different metals, each with a separate frangibility?

5.8 Or is 'link' a false metaphor?

5.9 But allowing that it is not, if a link breaks, wherein lies the responsibility for such breaking? On the links immediately on either side, or on the whole chain? But what do we mean by 'the whole chain'? How far do the limits of responsibility extend?

6.0 Or we might try to draw the responsibility more narrowly and apportion it more exactly. And not use equations and integers but instead express matters in traditional narrative terminology. So, for instance, if Tony

And there the photocopy – this version of a version – stopped. 'So, for instance, if Tony': end of the line, bottom of the page. If I hadn't immediately recognised Adrian's handwriting, I might have thought this cliffhanger a part of some elaborate fakery concocted by Veronica.

But I didn't want to think about her – not for as long as it was possible to avoid doing so. Instead I tried to concentrate on Adrian and what he was doing. I don't know how best to put this, but as I looked at that photocopied page I didn't feel as if I was examining some historical document – one, moreover, requiring considerable exegesis. No, I felt as if Adrian was present in the room again, beside me, breathing, thinking.

And how admirable he remained. I have at times tried

to imagine the despair which leads to suicide, attempted to conjure up the slew and slop of darkness in which only death appears as a pinprick of light: in other words, the exact opposite of the normal condition of life. But in this document – which I took, on the basis of this one page, to consist of Adrian's rational arguing towards his own suicide – the writer was using light in an attempt to reach greater light. Does that make sense?

I'm sure psychologists have somewhere made a graph of intelligence measured against age. Not a graph of wisdom, pragmatism, organisational skill, tactical nous – those things which, over time, blur our understanding of the matter. But a graph of pure intelligence. And my guess is that it would show we most of us peak between the ages of sixteen and twenty-five. Adrian's fragment brought me back to how he was at that age. When we had talked and argued, it was as if setting thoughts in order was what he had been designed to do, as if using his brain was as natural as an athlete using his muscles. And just as athletes often react to victory with a curious mixture of pride, disbelief and modesty – *I* did this, yet how did I do this? by myself? thanks to others? or did God do it for me? – so Adrian would take you along on the journey of his thought as if he himself didn't quite believe the ease with which he was travelling. He had entered some state of grace – but one that did not exclude. He made you feel you were his co-thinker, even if you said nothing. And it was very strange for me to feel this again, this companionship with one now dead but still more intelligent, for all my extra decades of life.

Not just pure, but also applied intelligence. I found myself comparing my life against Adrian's. The ability to see and examine himself; the ability to make moral decisions and act on them; the mental and physical courage of his suicide. 'He took his own life' is the phrase; but Adrian also took charge of his own life, he took command of it, he took it in his hands – and then out of them. How few of us – we that remain – can say that we have done the same? We muddle along, we let life happen to us, we gradually build up a store of memories. There is the question of accumulation, but not in the sense that Adrian meant, just the simple adding up and adding on of life. And as the poet pointed out, there is a difference between addition and increase.

Had my life increased, or merely added to itself? This was the question Adrian's fragment set off in me. There had been addition – and subtraction – in my life, but how much multiplication? And this gave me a sense of unease, of unrest.

'So, for instance, if Tony . . .' These words had a local, textual meaning, specific to forty years ago; and I might at some point discover that they contained, or led to, a rebuke, a criticism from my old clear-seeing, self-seeing friend. But for the moment I heard them with a wider reference – to the whole of my life. 'So, for instance, if Tony . . .' And in this register the words were practically complete in themselves and didn't need an explanatory main clause to follow. Yes indeed, if Tony had seen more clearly, acted more decisively, held to truer moral values, settled less easily for a passive peaceableness which he first called happiness and later contentment. If Tony hadn't been fearful, hadn't counted on the approval of others for his own self-approval . . . and so on, through a succession of hypotheticals leading to the final one: so, for instance, if Tony hadn't been Tony.

But Tony was and is Tony, a man who found comfort in his own doggedness. Letters to insurance companies, emails to Veronica. If you're going to bugger me about, then I'm going to bugger you about back. I carried on sending her emails more or less every other day, and now in a variety of tones, from jokey exhortations to 'Do the right thing, girl!', to questions about Adrian's broken-off sentence, to half-sincere enquiries about her own life. I wanted her to feel that I might be waiting whenever she clicked on her inbox; and I wanted her to know that even if she instantly deleted my messages, I would be aware that this was what she was doing, and not surprised, let alone hurt. And that I was there, waiting. 'Ti-*yi-yi-yime* is on my side, yes it is . . .' I didn't feel I was harassing her; I was just after what was mine. And then, one morning, I got a result.

'I'm coming up to town tomorrow, I'll meet you at 3 in the middle of the Wobbly Bridge.'

I'd never expected that. I thought everything would be done at arm's length, her methods being solicitors and silence. Maybe she'd had a change of mind. Or maybe I'd got under her skin. I'd been trying to, after all.

The Wobbly Bridge is the new footbridge across the Thames, linking St Paul's to Tate Modern. When it first opened, it used to shake a bit – either from the wind or the mass of people tramping across it, or both – and the British commentariat duly mocked the architects and engineers for not knowing what they were doing. I thought it beautiful. I also liked the way it wobbled. It seemed to me that we ought occasionally to be reminded of instability beneath our feet. Then they fixed it and it stopped wobbling, but the name stuck – at least for the time being. I wondered about Veronica's choice of location. Also if she'd keep me waiting, and from which side she'd arrive.

But she was there already. I recognised her from a distance, her height and stance being instantly familiar. Odd how the image of someone's posture always remains with you. And in her case – how can I put it? Can you stand impatiently? I don't mean she was hopping from one foot to the other; but an evident tenseness suggested she didn't want to be there.

I checked my watch. I was exactly on time. We looked at one another.

'You've lost your hair,' she said.

'It happens. At least it shows I'm not an alcoholic.'

'I didn't say you were. We'll sit on one of those benches.'

She headed off without waiting for an answer. She was walking swiftly, and I would have had to run a few steps to get alongside her. I didn't want to give her this pleasure, so followed a few paces behind to an empty bench facing the Thames. I couldn't tell which way the tide was running, as a whippy crosswind stirred the water's surface. Above, the sky was grey. There were few tourists; a rollerblader rattled past behind us.

'Why do people think you're an alcoholic?'

'They don't.'

'Then why did you bring it up?'

'I didn't bring it up. You said I'd lost my hair. And it

happens to be a fact that if you're a very heavy drinker, something in the booze stops your hair falling out.'

'Is that true?'

'Well, can you think of a bald alcoholic?'

'I've got better things to do with my time.'

I glanced at her and thought: You haven't changed, but I have. And yet, oddly, these conversational tactics made me almost nostalgic. Almost. At the same time, I thought: You look a bit whiskery. She was wearing a utilitarian tweed skirt and a rather shabby blue mackintosh; her hair, even allowing for the breeze off the river, seemed unkempt. It was the same length as forty years earlier, but heavily streaked with grey. Or rather, it was grey streaked with the original brown. Margaret used to say that women often made the mistake of keeping their hair in the style they adopted when they were at their most attractive. They hung on long after it became inappropriate, all because they were afraid of the big cut. This certainly seemed to be the case with Veronica. Or maybe she just didn't care.

'So?' she said.

'So?' I repeated.

'You asked to meet.'

'Did I?'

'You mean you didn't?'

'If you say I did, I must have.'

'Well, is it yes or no?' she asked, getting to her feet and standing, yes, impatiently.

I deliberately didn't react. I didn't suggest she sit down, nor did I stand up myself. She could leave if she wanted – and she would, so there was no point trying to hold her back. She was gazing out over the water. She had three moles on the side of her neck – did I remember them or not? Each, now, had a long whisker growing out of it, and the light caught these filaments of hair.

Very well then, no small talk, no history, no nostalgia. To business.

'Are you going to let me have Adrian's diary?'

'I can't,' she replied, without looking at me.

'Why not?'

'I burnt it.'

First theft, then arson, I thought, with a spurt of anger. But I told myself to keep treating her like an insurance company. So, as neutrally as possible, I merely asked,

'For what reason?'

Her cheek twitched, but I couldn't tell if it was a smile or a wince.

'People shouldn't read other people's diaries.'

'Your mother must have read it. And so must you, to decide which page to send me.' No answer. Try another tack. 'By the way, how did that sentence continue? You know the one: "So, for instance, if Tony . . ."?'

A shrug and a frown. 'People shouldn't read other people's diaries,' she repeated. 'But you can read this if you like.'

She pulled an envelope from her raincoat pocket, handed it to me, turned, and walked off.

When I got home, I checked through my sent emails and, of course, I'd never asked for a meeting. Well, not in so many words, anyway.

I remembered my initial reaction to seeing the phrase 'blood money' on my screen. I'd said to myself: But nobody got killed. I'd just been thinking about Veronica and me. I hadn't considered Adrian.

Another thing I realised: there was a mistake, or a

statistical anomaly, in Margaret's theory of clear-edged versus mysterious women; or rather, in the second part of it, about men being attracted to either one sort or the other. I'd been attracted to both Veronica and Margaret.

I remember a period in late adolescence when my mind would make itself drunk with images of adventurousness. This is how it will be when I grow up. I shall go there, do this, discover that, love her, and then her and her and her. I shall live as people in novels live and have lived. Which ones I was not sure, only that passion and danger, ecstasy and despair (but then more ecstasy) would be in attendance. However . . . who said that thing about 'the littleness of life that art exaggerates'? There was a moment in my late twenties when I admitted that my adventurousness had long since petered out. I would never do those things adolescence had dreamt about. Instead, I mowed my lawn, I took holidays, I had my life.

But time . . . how time first grounds us and then confounds us. We thought we were being mature when we were only being safe. We imagined we were being responsible but were only being cowardly. What we called realism turned out to be a way of avoiding things rather than facing them. Time . . . give us enough time and our best-supported decisions will seem wobbly, our certainties whimsical.

I didn't open the envelope Veronica gave me for a day and a half. I waited because I knew she would expect me not to wait, to have my thumb at the flap before she was out of sight. But I knew the envelope was hardly likely to contain what I wanted: for instance, the key to a left-luggage locker where I would find Adrian's diary. At the same time, I wasn't convinced by her prim line about not reading other people's diaries. I thought her quite capable of arson to punish me for ancient wrongs and failings, but not in defence of some hastily erected principle of correct behaviour.

It puzzled me that she had suggested a meeting. Why not use Royal Mail and so avoid an encounter which she clearly found distasteful? Why this face-to-face? Because she was curious to set eyes on me again after all these years, even if it made her shudder? I rather doubted it. I ran through the ten minutes or so we had spent in one another's company – the location, the change of location, the anxiety to be gone from both, what was said and what was unsaid. Eventually, I came up with a theory. If she didn't need the meeting for what she had done – which was give me the envelope – then she needed it for what she had said. Which was that she had burnt Adrian's diary. And why did she have to put that into words by the grey Thamesside? Because it was deniable. She didn't want the corroboration of the printed-out email. If she could falsely assert that I was the one who had asked for a meeting, it wouldn't be a stretch for her to deny that she had ever admitted arson.

Having arrived at this tentative explanation, I waited until the evening, had my supper, poured an extra glass of wine, and sat down with the envelope. It didn't have my name on it: perhaps more evidence of deniability? Of course I didn't give it to him. Nor did I even meet him. He's just an email pest, a fantasist, a bald cyberstalker.

I could tell, from the band of grey shading to black round the edge of the first page, that here was another photocopy. What was it with her? Did she never deal in authentic documents? Then I noticed the date at the top, and the handwriting: my own, as it used to be, all those years ago. 'Dear Adrian,' the letter began. I read it through, got to my feet, took my glass of wine, poured it rather splashily back into the bottle, and made myself a very large whisky.

How often do we tell our own life story? How often do we adjust, embellish, make sly cuts? And the longer life goes on, the fewer are those around to challenge our account, to remind us that our life is not our life, merely the story we have told about our life. Told to others, but – mainly – to ourselves.

Dear Adrian – or rather, Dear Adrian and Veronica (hello, Bitch, and welcome to this letter),

Well you certainly deserve one another and I wish you much joy. I hope you get so involved that the mutual damage will be permanent. I hope you regret the day I introduced you. And I hope that when you break up, as you inevitably will – I give you six months, which your shared pride will extend to a year, all the better for fucking you up, says I – you are left with a lifetime of bitterness that will poison your subsequent relationships. Part of me hopes you'll have a child, because I'm a great believer in time's revenge, yea unto the next generation and the next. See Great Art. But revenge must be on the right people, i.e. you two (and you're not great art, just a cartoonist's doodle). So I don't wish you that. It would be unjust to inflict on some innocent foetus the prospect of discovering that it was the fruit of your loins, if you'll excuse the poeticism. So keep rolling the Durex on to his spindly cock, Veronica. Or perhaps you haven't let him go that far yet?

Still, enough of the courtesies. I have just a few precise things to say to each of you.

Adrian: you already know she's a cockteaser, of course – though I expect you told yourself she was engaged in a Struggle With Her Principles, which you as a philosopher would employ your grey cells to help her overcome. If she hasn't let you Go All The Way yet, I suggest you break up with her, and she'll be round your place with sodden knickers and a three-pack, eager to give it away. But cockteasing is also a metaphor: she is someone who will manipulate your inner self while holding hers back from you. I leave a precise diagnosis to the headshrinkers – which might vary according to the day of the week – and merely note her inability to imagine anyone else's feelings or emotional life. Even her own mother warned me against her. If I were you, I'd check things out with Mum – ask her about damage a long way back. Of course, you'll have to do this behind Veronica's back, because boy is that girl a control freak. Oh, and she's also a snob, as you must be aware, who only took up with you because you were soon to have BA Cantab after your name. Remember how much you despised Brother Jack and his posh friends? Is that who you want to run with now? But don't forget: give her time, and she'll look down on you just as she looks down on me.

Veronica: interesting, that joint letter. Your malice mixed with his priggishness. Quite a marriage of talents. Like your sense of social superiority versus his sense of intellectual superiority. But don't think you can outsmart Adrian as you (for a time) outsmarted me. I can see your tactics – isolate him, cut him off from his old friends, make him dependent on you, etc., etc. That might work in the short term. But in the long? It's just a question of whether you can get pregnant before he discovers you're a bore. And even if you do nail him down, you can look forward to a lifetime of having your logic corrected, to breakfast-table pedantry and stifled yawns at your airs and graces. I can't do anything to you now, but time can. Time will tell. It always does.

Compliments of the season to you, and may the acid rain fall on your joint and anointed heads.

Tony

Whisky, I find, helps clarity of thought. And reduces pain. It has the additional virtue of making you drunk or, if taken in sufficient quantity, very drunk. I reread this letter several times. I could scarcely deny its authorship or its ugliness. All I could plead was that I had been its author then, but was not its author now. Indeed, I didn't recognise that part of myself from which the letter came. But perhaps this was simply further self-deception.

At first, I thought mainly about me, and how – what – I'd been: chippy, jealous and malign. Also about my attempt to undermine their relationship. At least I'd failed in this, since Veronica's mother had assured me the last months of Adrian's life had been happy. Not that this let me off the hook. My younger self had come back to shock my older self with what that self had been, or was, or was sometimes capable of being. And only recently I'd been going on about how the witnesses to our lives decrease, and with them our essential corroboration. Now I had some all too unwelcome corroboration of what I was, or had been. If only this had been the document Veronica had set light to.

Next I thought about her. Not about how she might have felt on first reading the letter – I would come back to this – but why she had handed it over. Of course, she wanted to point out what a shit I was. But it was more than this, I decided: given our current stand-off, it was also a tactical move, a warning. If I tried to make any legal fuss about the diary, this would be part of her defence. I would be my very own character witness.

Then I thought about Adrian. My old friend who had killed himself. And this had been the last communication he had ever received from me. A libel on his character and an attempt to destroy the first and last love affair of his life. And when I had written that time would tell, I had under-estimated, or rather miscalculated: time was telling not against them, it was telling against me.

And finally I remembered the postcard I'd sent Adrian as a holding response to his letter. The fake-cool one about everything being fine, old bean. The card was of the Clifton Suspension Bridge. From which a number of people every year jump to their deaths.

The next day, when I was sober, I thought again about the three of us, and about time's many paradoxes. For instance: that when we are young and sensitive, we are also at our most hurtful; whereas when the blood begins to slow, when we feel less sharply, when we are more armoured and have learnt how to bear hurt, we tread more carefully. Nowadays I might try to get under Veronica's skin, but I would never try to flay it from her bit by bloody bit.

It was not, in retrospect, cruel of them to warn me that they were an item. It was just the timing of it, and the fact that Veronica had seemed to be behind the whole idea. Why had I reacted by going nuclear? Hurt pride, pre-exam stress, isolation? Excuses, all of them. And no, it wasn't shame I now felt, or guilt, but something rarer in my life and stronger than both: remorse. A feeling which is more complicated, curdled, and primeval. Whose chief characteristic is that nothing can be done about it: too much time has passed, too much damage has been done, for amends to be made. Even so, forty years on, I sent Veronica an email apologising for my letter.

Then I thought more about Adrian. From the beginning, he had always seen more clearly than the rest of us. While we luxuriated in the doldrums of adolescence, imagining our routine discontent to be an original response to the human condition, Adrian was already looking farther ahead and wider around. He felt life more clearly too – even, perhaps especially, when he came to decide that it wasn't worth the candle. Compared to him, I had always been a muddler, unable to learn much from the few lessons life provided me with. In my terms, I settled for the realities of life, and submitted to its necessities: if this, then that, and so the years passed. In Adrian's terms, I gave up on life, gave up on examining it, took it as it came. And so, for the first time, I began to feel a more general remorse – a feeling somewhere between self-pity and self-hatred – about my whole life. All of it. I had lost the friends of my youth. I had lost the love of my wife. I had abandoned the ambitions I had entertained. I had wanted life not to bother me too much, and had succeeded – and how pitiful that was.

Average, that's what I'd been, ever since I left school. Average at university and work; average in friendship, loyalty, love; average, no doubt, at sex. There was a survey of British motorists a few years ago which showed that ninety-five per cent of those polled thought they were 'better than average' drivers. But by the law of averages, we're most of us bound to be average. Not that this brought any comfort. The word resounded. Average at life; average at truth; morally average. Veronica's first reaction to seeing me again had been to point out that I'd lost my hair. That was the least of it.

The email she sent in reply to my apology read: 'You just don't get it, do you? But then you never did.' I could hardly complain. Even if I found myself pathetically wishing she'd used my name in one of her two sentences.

I wondered how Veronica had retained possession of my letter. Did Adrian leave her all his stuff in his will? I didn't even know if he'd made one. Perhaps he'd kept it inside his diary, and she'd found it there. No, I wasn't thinking clearly. If that's where it had been, Mrs Ford would have seen it – and then she certainly wouldn't have left me five hundred pounds.

I wondered why Veronica had bothered to answer my email, given that she affected to despise me completely. Well, maybe she didn't.

I wondered if Veronica had punished Brother Jack for passing on her email address.

I wondered if, all those years ago, her words 'It doesn't feel right' were simply a politeness. Perhaps she hadn't wanted to sleep with me because the sexual contact we'd had during the time she was deciding just wasn't enjoyable enough. I wondered if I'd been awkward, pushy, selfish. Not if, how.

Margaret sat and listened through the quiche and salad, then the pannacotta with fruit coulis, as I described my contact with Jack, the page of Adrian's diary, the meeting on the bridge, the contents of my letter and my feelings of remorse. She put her coffee cup back on its saucer with a slight click.

'You're not still in love with the Fruitcake.'

'No, I don't think I am.'

'Tony, that wasn't a question. It was a statement.'

I looked across at her fondly. She knew me better than anyone else in the world. And still wanted to have lunch with me. And let me go on and on about myself. I smiled at her, in a way she also doubtless knew too well.

'One of these days I'll surprise you,' I said.

'You do still. You have today.'

'Yes, but I want to surprise you in a way that makes you think better of me rather than worse.'

'I don't think the worse of you. I don't even think the worse of the Fruitcake, though admittedly my estimation of her has always been below sea level.'

Margaret doesn't do triumphalism; she also knew that she didn't have to point out that I'd ignored her advice. I think she quite likes being a sympathetic ear, and also quite likes being reminded why she's glad not to be married to me any more. I don't mean that in a bitchy sense. I just think it's the case.

'Can I ask you something?'

'You always do,' she replied.

'Did you leave me because of me?'

'No,' she said. 'I left you because of us.'

Susie and I get on fine, as I have a tendency to repeat. And that will do as a statement I would happily swear to in a court of law. She's thirty-three, maybe thirty-four. Yes, thirty-four. We haven't had any sort of falling-out since I sat in the front row of an oak-panelled municipal room and then did my job as a witness. I remember thinking at the time that I was signing off on her – or, more exactly, signing myself off. Duty done, only child safely seen to the temporary harbour of marriage. Now all you have to do is not get Alzheimer's and remember to leave her such money as you have. And you could try to do better than your parents by dying when the money will actually be of use to her. That'd be a start.

If Margaret and I had stayed together, I dare say I would have been allowed to be more of a doting grandfather. It's not surprising Margaret's been more use. Susie didn't want to leave the kids with me because she didn't think I was capable, despite all the nappies I'd changed and so on. 'You can take Lucas to watch football when he's older,' she once told me. Ah, the rheumy-eyed grandpa on the terraces inducting the lad into the mysteries of soccer: how to loathe people wearing different coloured shirts, how to feign injury, how to blow your snot on to the pitch – See, son, you press hard on one nostril to close it, and explode the green stuff out of the other. How to be vain and overpaid and have your best years behind you before you've even

understood what life's about. Oh yes, I look forv.
taking Lucas to the football.

But Susie doesn't notice that I dislike the game – or
dislike what it's become. She's practical about emotions,
Susie is. Gets that from her mother. So my emotions as
they actually are don't concern her. She prefers to assume
that I have certain feelings and operate according to that
assumption. At some level, she blames me for the divorce.
As in: since it was all her mother's doing, it was obviously
all her father's fault.

Does character develop over time? In novels, of course it
does: otherwise there wouldn't be much of a story. But in
life? I sometimes wonder. Our attitudes and opinions change,
we develop new habits and eccentricities; but that's something different, more like decoration. Perhaps character
resembles intelligence, except that character peaks a little
later: between twenty and thirty, say. And after that, we're
just stuck with what we've got. We're on our own. If so,
that would explain a lot of lives, wouldn't it? And also – if
this isn't too grand a word – our tragedy.

'The question of accumulation,' Adrian had written. You
put money on a horse, it wins, and your winnings go on
to the next horse in the next race, and so on. Your winnings
accumulate. But do your losses? Not at the racetrack – there,
you just lose your original stake. But in life? Perhaps here
different rules apply. You bet on a relationship, it fails; you
go on to the next relationship, it fails too: and maybe what
you lose is not two simple minus sums but the multiple of

hat's what it feels like, anyway. Life isn't
ubtraction. There's also the accumulation,
n, of loss, of failure.

gment also refers to the question of respon-
er there's a chain of it, or whether we draw
th... more narrowly. I'm all for drawing it narrowly.
Sorry, n.. you can't blame your dead parents, or having
brothers and sisters, or not having them, or your genes, or
society, or whatever – not in normal circumstances. Start
with the notion that yours is the sole responsibility unless
there's powerful evidence to the contrary. Adrian was much
cleverer than me – he used logic where I use common
sense – but we came, I think, to more or less the same
conclusion.

Not that I can understand everything he wrote. I stared
at those equations in his diary without much illumination
coming my way. But then I was never any good at maths.

I don't envy Adrian his death, but I envy him the clarity
of his life. Not just because he saw, thought, felt and acted
more clearly than the rest of us; but also because of when
he died. I don't mean any of that First World War rubbish:
'Cut down in the flower of youth' – a line still being
churned out by our headmaster at the time of Robson's
suicide – and 'They shall grow not old as we that are left
grow old.' Most of the rest of us haven't minded growing
old. It's always better than the alternative in my book. No,
what I mean is this. When you are in your twenties, even
if you're confused and uncertain about your aims and
purposes, you have a strong sense of what life itself is, and
of what you in life are, and might become. Later . . . later

there is more uncertainty, more overlapping, more back-tracking, more false memories. Back then, you can remember your short life in its entirety. Later, the memory becomes a thing of shreds and patches. It's a bit like the black box aeroplanes carry to record what happens in a crash. If nothing goes wrong, the tape erases itself. So if you do crash, it's obvious why you did; if you don't, then the log of your journey is much less clear.

Or, to put it another way. Someone once said that his favourite times in history were when things were collapsing, because that meant something new was being born. Does this make any sense if we apply it to our individual lives? To die when something new is being born – even if that something new is our very own self? Because just as all political and historical change sooner or later disappoints, so does adulthood. So does life. Sometimes I think the purpose of life is to reconcile us to its eventual loss by wearing us down, by proving, however long it takes, that life isn't all it's cracked up to be.

Imagine someone, late at night, a bit drunk, writing a letter to an old girlfriend. He addresses the envelope, puts on a stamp, finds his coat, walks to the postbox, shoves the letter into it, walks home and goes to bed. Most likely, he wouldn't do all that last bit, would he? He'd leave the letter out for posting in the morning. And then, quite possibly, have second thoughts. So there's a lot to be said for email, for its spontaneity, immediacy, truth to feeling, even its gaffes. My thinking – if that isn't too grand a word for it – went like this: why take Margaret's word for it? – she wasn't even there, and can only have her prejudices. So I sent an email to Veronica. I headed it 'Question', and asked her this: 'Do you think I was in love with you back then?' I signed it with my initial and hit Send before I could change my mind.

The last thing I expected was a reply the next morning. This time she hadn't deleted my subject heading. Her reply read: 'If you need to ask the question, then the answer is no. V.'

It perhaps says something of my state of mind that I found this response normal, indeed encouraging.

It perhaps says something else that my reaction was to ring up Margaret and tell her of the exchange. There was a silence, then my ex-wife said quietly, 'Tony, you're on your own now.'

You can put it another way, of course; you always can. So, for example, there is the question of contempt, and our response to it. Brother Jack gives me a supercilious wink, and forty years later I use what charm I have – no, let's not exaggerate: I use a certain false politeness – to get information out of him. And then, instantly, I betray him. My contempt in exchange for your contempt. Even if, as I now admit, what he actually felt towards me back then might have been just an amused lack of interest. Here comes my sister's latest – well, there was one before him, and there'll doubtless be another along soon. No need to examine this passing specimen too closely. But I – I – felt it as contempt at the time, remembered it as such, and delivered the feeling back.

And maybe with Veronica I was trying to do something more: not return her contempt, but overcome it. You can see the attraction of this. Because rereading that letter of mine, feeling its harshness and aggression, came as a profound and intimate shock. If she hadn't felt contempt for me before, she'd have been bound to after Adrian showed her my words. And bound also to carry that resentment down the years, and use it to justify withholding, even destroying, Adrian's diary.

I was saying, confidently, how the chief characteristic of remorse is that nothing can be done about it: that the time has passed for apology or amends. But what if I'm wrong? What if by some means remorse can be made to flow backwards, can be transmuted into simple guilt, then apologised for, and then forgiven? What if you can prove you weren't the bad guy she took you for, and she is willing to accept your proof?

Or perhaps my motive came from a totally opposite direction, and wasn't about the past but the future. Like most people, I have superstitions attached to the taking of a journey. We may know that flying is statistically safer than walking to the corner shop. Even so, before going away I do things like pay bills, clear off correspondence, phone someone close.

'Susie, I'm off tomorrow.'

'Yes, I know, Dad. You told me.'

'Did I?'

'Yes.'

'Well, just to say goodbye.'

'Sorry, Dad, the kids were making a noise. What was that?'

'Oh, nothing, give them my love.'

You're doing it for yourself, of course. You're wanting to leave that final memory, and make it a pleasant one. You want to be well thought of – in case your plane turns out to be the one that's less safe than walking to the corner shop.

And if this is how we behave before a five-night winter break in Mallorca, then why should there not be a broader process at work towards the end of life, as that final journey – the motorised trundle through the crematorium's curtains – approaches? Don't think ill of me, remember me well. Tell people you were fond of me, that you loved me, that I wasn't a bad guy. Even if, perhaps, none of this was the case.

I opened an old photo album and looked at the picture she'd asked me to take in Trafalgar Square. 'One with your friends.' Alex and Colin are putting on rather exaggerated this-is-for-the-historical-record faces, Adrian looks normally serious, while Veronica – as I had never before noticed – is turning slightly in towards him. Not looking up at him, but equally not looking at the camera. In other words, not looking at me. I'd got jealous that day. I'd wanted to introduce her to my friends, wanted her to like them, and them to like her, though of course not more than any of them liked me. Which might have been a juvenile, as well as an unrealistic, expectation. So when she kept asking Adrian questions, I got petulant; and when, later, in the hotel bar, Adrian had slagged off Brother Jack and his chums, I felt better immediately.

I briefly considered tracking down Alex and Colin. I imagined asking for their memories and their corroboration. But they were hardly central to the story; I didn't expect their memories to be better than mine. And what if their corroboration proved the opposite of helpful? Actually, Tony, I suppose it won't do any harm to speak the truth after all these years, but Adrian was always very cutting about you behind your back. Oh, how interesting. Yes, we both noticed that. He said you weren't either as nice or as clever as you thought you were. I see; anything else? Yes, he said the way you made it obvious that you considered yourself his closest friend – closer, anyway, than the two of us – was absurd and incomprehensible. Right, is that all? Not quite: anyone could see that what's-her-name was stringing you along until something better turned up. Didn't you notice the way she was flirting with Adrian that day we all met? The two of us were pretty shocked by it. She practically had her tongue in his ear.

No, they wouldn't be any help. And Mrs Ford was dead. And Brother Jack was off the scene. The only possible witness, the only corroborator, was Veronica.

I said I wanted to get under her skin, didn't I? It's an odd expression, and one that always makes me think of Margaret's way of roasting a chicken. She'd gently loosen the skin from the breast and thighs, then slip butter and herbs underneath. Tarragon, probably. Perhaps some garlic as well, I'm not sure. I've never tried it myself, then or since; my fingers are too clumsy, and I imagine them ripping the skin.

Margaret told me of a French way of doing this which is even fancier. They put slices of black truffle under the skin – and do you know what they call it? Chicken in Half-Mourning. I suppose the recipe dates from the time people used to wear nothing but black for a few months, grey for another few months, and only slowly return to the colours of life. Full-, Half-, Quarter-Mourning. I don't know if those were the terms, but I know the gradations of dress were fully tabulated. Nowadays, how long do people wear mourning? Half a day in most cases – just long enough for the funeral or cremation and the drinks afterwards.

Sorry, that's a bit off the track. I wanted to get under her skin, that's what I said, didn't I? Did I mean what I thought I meant by it, or something else? 'I've Got You Under My Skin' – that's a love song, isn't it?

I don't want to blame Margaret at all. Not in the slightest. But, to put it simply, if I was on my own, then who did I have? I hesitated for a few days before sending Veronica a new email. In it, I asked about her parents. Was her father still alive? Had her mother's end been gentle? I added that, though I'd met them only once, I had good memories. Well, that was fifty per cent true. I didn't really understand why I asked these questions. I suppose I wanted to do something normal, or at least pretend that something was normal even if it wasn't. When you're young – when I was young – you want your emotions to be like the ones you read about in books. You want them to overturn your life, create and define a new reality. Later, I think, you want them to do something milder, something more practical: you want them to support your life as it is and has become. You want them to tell you that things are OK. And is there anything wrong with that?

Veronica's reply was a surprise and a relief. She didn't treat my questions as impertinent. It was almost as if she was pleased to be asked. Her father had been dead some thirty-five years and more. His drinking had got worse and worse; oesophageal cancer was the result. I paused at that, feeling guilty that my first words to Veronica on the Wobbly Bridge had been flippant ones about bald alcoholics.

After his death, her mother had sold the house in Chislehurst and moved up to London. She did art classes, started smoking, and took in lodgers, even though she'd been left well provided for. She had remained in good health until a year or so ago, when her memory began to fail. A small stroke was suspected. Then she started putting the tea in the fridge and the eggs in the breadbin, that sort of thing. Once she nearly set the house on fire by leaving a cigarette burning. She remained cheerful throughout, until she suddenly went downhill. The last months had been a struggle, and no, her end had not been gentle, though it had been a mercy.

I reread this email several times. I was looking for traps, ambiguities, implied insults. There were none – unless straightforwardness itself can be a trap. It was an ordinary, sad story – all too familiar – and simply told.

When you start forgetting things – I don't mean Alzheimer's, just the predictable consequence of ageing – there are different ways to react. You can sit there and try to force your memory into giving up the name of that acquaintance, flower, train station, astronaut . . . Or you admit failure and take practical steps with reference books and the internet. Or you can just let it go – forget about remembering – and then sometimes you find that the mislaid fact surfaces an hour or a day later, often in those long waking nights that age imposes. Well, we all learn this, those of us who forget things.

But we also learn something else: that the brain doesn't like being typecast. Just when you think everything is a matter of decrease, of subtraction and division, your brain, your memory, may surprise you. As if it's saying: Don't imagine you can rely on some comforting process of gradual decline – life's *much* more complicated than that. And so the brain will throw you scraps from time to time, even disengage those familiar memory-loops. That's what, to my consternation, I found happening to me now. I began to remember, with no particular order or sense of significance, long-buried details of that distant weekend with the Ford family. My attic room had a view across roofs to a wood; from below I could hear a clock striking the hour precisely five minutes late. Mrs Ford flipped the broken, cooked egg into the waste bin with an expression of concern – for it, not me. Her husband tried to get me to drink brandy after dinner, and when I refused, asked if I were a man or a mouse. Brother Jack addressed Mrs Ford as 'the Mother', as in 'When does the Mother think there might be fodder for the starving troops?' And on the second night, Veronica did more than just come upstairs with me. She said, 'I'm going to walk Tony to his room,' and took my hand in front of the family. Brother Jack said, 'And what does the Mother think of that?' But the Mother only smiled. My goodnights to the family that evening were hasty as I could feel an erection coming on. We walked slowly up to my bedroom, where Veronica backed me against the door, kissed me on the mouth and said into my ear, 'Sleep the sleep of the wicked.' And approximately forty seconds later, I now remember, I was wanking into the little washbasin and sluicing my sperm down the house's pipework.

On a whim, I Googled Chislehurst. And discovered that there'd never been a St Michael's church in the town. So Mr Ford's guided tour as he drove us along must have been fanciful – some private joke, or way of stringing me along. I doubt very much there'd been a Café Royal either. Then I went on Google Earth, swooping and zooming around the town. But the house I was looking for didn't seem to exist any more.

The other night, I allowed myself another drink, turned on my computer, and called up the only Veronica in my address book. I suggested we meet again. I apologised for anything I might have done to make things awkward on the previous occasion. I promised that I didn't want to talk about her mother's will. This was true, too; though it wasn't until I wrote that sentence that I realised I had barely given Adrian or his diary a thought for quite a few days.

'Is this about closing the circle?' came her reply.

'I don't know,' I wrote back. 'But it can't do any harm, can it?'

She didn't answer that question, but at the time I didn't notice or mind.

I don't know why, but part of me thought she'd suggest meeting on the bridge again. Either that, or somewhere snug and promisingly personal: a forgotten pub, a quiet lunchroom, even the bar at the Charing Cross Hotel. She chose the brasserie on the third floor of John Lewis in Oxford Street.

Actually, this had its convenient side: I needed a few metres of cord for restringing a blind, some kettle descaler, and a set of those patches you iron on the inside of trousers when the knee splits. It's hard to find this stuff locally any more: where I live, most of those useful little shops have long been turned into cafés or estate agents.

On the train up to town, there was a girl sitting opposite me, plugged into earphones, eyes closed, impervious to the world outside, moving her head to music only she could hear. And suddenly, a complete memory came to me: of Veronica dancing. Yes, she didn't dance – that's what I said – but there'd been one evening in my room when she got all mischievous and started pulling out my pop records.

'Put one on and let me see you dance,' she said.

I shook my head. 'Takes two to tango.'

'OK, you show me and I'll join in.'

So I stacked the autochanger spindle with 45s, moved across to her, did a skeleton-loosening shrug, half-closed my eyes, as if respecting her privacy, and went for it. Basic male display behaviour of the period, determinedly individualistic while actually dependent on a strict imitation of prevailing norms: the head-jerking and the foot-prancing, the shoulder-twisting and the pelvis-jabbing, with the bonus of ecstatically raised arms and occasional grunting noises. After a bit, I opened my eyes, expecting her to be still sitting on the floor and laughing at me. But there she was, leaping about in a way that made me suspect she'd been to ballet classes, her hair all over her face and her calves tense and full of strut. I watched her for a bit, unsure if she was sending me up or genuinely grooving along to the Moody Blues. Actually, I didn't care – I was enjoying myself and feeling a small victory. This went on for a while; then I moved closer to her as Ned Miller's

'From a Jack to a King' gave way to Bob Lind singing 'Elusive Butterfly'. But she didn't notice and, twirling, bumped into me, nearly losing her balance. I caught her and held her.

'You see, it's not that difficult.'

'Oh, I never thought it was difficult,' she replied. 'Good. Yes. Thank you,' she said formally, then went and sat down. 'You carry on if you want to. I've had enough.'

Still, she had danced.

I did my errands in the haberdashery, kitchen and curtain departments, then went to the brasserie. I was ten minutes early but of course Veronica was already there, head down, reading, confident that I would find her. As I put my bags down, she looked up and half-smiled. I thought: you don't look so wild and whiskery after all.

'I'm still bald,' I said.

She held on to a quarter-smile.

'What are you reading?'

She turned the cover of her paperback towards me. Something by Stefan Zweig.

'So you've finally got to the end of the alphabet. Can't be anyone left after him.' Why was I suddenly nervous? I was talking like a twenty-year-old again. Also, I hadn't read any Stefan Zweig.

'I'm having the pasta,' she said.

Well, at least it wasn't a put-down.

While I inspected the menu, she carried on reading. The table looked out over a criss-cross of escalators. People going up, people going down; everyone buying something.

'On the train up I was remembering when you danced. In my room. In Bristol.'

I expected her to contradict me, or take some indecipherable offence. But she only said, 'I wonder why you remembered that.' And with this moment of corroboration, I began to feel a return of confidence. She was more smartly dressed this time; her hair was under control and seemed less grey. She somehow managed to look – to my eye – both twentyish and sixtyish at the same time.

'So,' I said, 'how've the last forty years been treating you?'

She looked at me. 'You first.'

I told her the story of my life. The version I tell myself, the account that stands up. She asked about 'those two friends of yours I once met', without, it seemed, being able to name them. I said how I'd lost touch with Colin and Alex. Then I told her about Margaret and Susie and grandparenthood, while batting away Margaret's whisper in my head of 'How's the Fruitcake?' I talked of my working life, and retirement, and keeping busy, and the winter breaks I took – this year I was thinking of St Petersburg in the snow for a change . . . I tried to sound content with my life but not complacent. I was in the middle of describing my grandchildren when she looked up, drank her coffee in one draught, put some money on the table and stood up. I started to reach for my own stuff when she said,

'No, you stay and finish yours.'

I was determined not to do anything which might cause offence, so I sat down again.

'Well, your turn next,' I said. Meaning: her life.

'Turn for what?' she asked, but was gone before I could reply.

Yes, I knew what she'd done. She'd managed to spend an hour in my company without divulging a single fact, let alone secret, about herself. Where she lived and how, whether she lived with anyone, or had children. On her wedding finger she wore a red glass ring, which was as enigmatic as the rest of her. But I didn't mind; indeed, I found myself reacting as if I'd been on a first date with someone and escaped without doing anything catastrophic. But of course it wasn't at all like that. After a first date you don't sit on a train and find your head flooded with the forgotten truth about your shared sex life forty years previously. How attracted to one another we had been; how light she felt on my lap; how exciting it always was; how, even though we weren't having 'full sex', all the elements of it – the lust, the tenderness, the candour, the trust – were there anyway. And how part of me hadn't minded not 'going the whole way', didn't mind the bouts of apocalyptic wanking after I'd seen her home, didn't mind sleeping in my single bed, alone except for my memories and a swiftly returning erection. This acceptance of less than others had was also due to fear, of course: fear of pregnancy, fear of saying or doing the wrong thing, fear of an overwhelming closeness I couldn't handle.

The next week was very quiet. I restrung my blind, descaled the kettle, mended the split in an old pair of jeans. Susie didn't call. Margaret, I knew, would be silent unless and until I got in touch with her. And then what would she expect? Apology, grovelling? No, she wasn't punitive; she'd always accept a rueful grin on my part as acknowledgement of her greater wisdom. But that might not be the case this time. In fact, I might not be seeing Margaret for a while.

Part of me felt distantly, quietly bad about her. At first I couldn't make any sense of this: she was the one who had told me I was now on my own. But then I had a memory from a long way back, from the early years of our marriage. Some chap at work gave a party and invited me along; Margaret didn't want to come. I flirted with a girl and she flirted back. Well, a bit more than flirting – though still way below even infra-sex – but I put a lid on it as soon as I sobered up. Yet it left me feeling excitement and guilt in equal proportions. And now, I realised, I was feeling something similar again. It took me some time to get this straight. Eventually I said to myself: Right, so you're feeling guilt towards your ex-wife, who divorced you twenty years ago, and excitement towards an old girlfriend you haven't seen in forty years. Who said there were no surprises left in life?

I didn't want to press Veronica. I thought I'd wait for her to get in touch this time. I checked my inbox rather too assiduously. Of course, I wasn't expecting a great effusion, but hoped, perhaps, for a polite message that it had been nice to see me properly after all these years.

Well, perhaps it hadn't been. Perhaps she'd gone on a trip. Perhaps her server was down. Who said that thing about the eternal hopefulness of the human heart? You know how you read those stories from time to time about what the papers like to call 'late-flowering love'? Usually about some old codger and codgeress in a retirement home? Both widowed, grinning through their dentures while holding arthritic hands? Often, they still talk what seems the inappropriate language of young love. 'As soon as I set eyes on him/her, I knew he/she was the one for me' – that sort of line. Part of me is always touched and wants to cheer; but another part is wary and baffled. Why go through that stuff all over again? Don't you know the rule: once bitten, twice bitten? But now, I found myself in revolt against my own . . . what? Conventionality, lack of imagination, expectation of disappointment? Also, I thought, I still have my own teeth.

That night a group of us went to Minsterworth in quest of the Severn Bore. Veronica had been alongside me. My brain must have erased it from the record, but now I knew it for a fact. She was there with me. We sat on a damp blanket on a damp riverside holding hands; she had brought a flask of hot chocolate. Innocent days. Moonlight caught the breaking wave as it approached. The others whooped at its arrival, and whooped off after it, chasing into the night with a scatter of intersecting torchbeams. Alone, she and I talked about how impossible things sometimes happened, things you wouldn't believe unless you'd witnessed them for yourself. Our mood was thoughtful, sombre even, rather than ecstatic.

At least, that's how I remember it now. Though if you were to put me in a court of law, I doubt I'd stand up to cross-examination very well. 'And yet you claim this memory was suppressed for forty years?' 'Yes.' 'And only surfaced just recently?' 'Yes.' 'Are you able to account for why it surfaced?' 'Not really.' 'Then let me put it to you, Mr Webster, that this supposed incident is an entire figment of your imagination, constructed to justify some romantic attachment which you appear to have been nurturing towards my client, a presumption which, the court should know, my client finds utterly repugnant.' 'Yes, perhaps. But –' 'But what, Mr Webster?' 'But we don't love many people in this life. One, two, three? And sometimes we don't recognise the fact until it's too late. Except that it isn't necessarily too late. Did you read that story about late-flowering love in an old people's home in Barnstaple?' 'Oh please, Mr Webster, spare us your sentimental lucubrations. This is a court of law, which deals with fact. What exactly are the facts in the case?'

I could only reply that I think – I theorise – that something – something else – happens to the memory over time. For years you survive with the same loops, the same facts and the same emotions. I press a button marked Adrian or Veronica, the tape runs, the usual stuff spools out. The events reconfirm the emotions – resentment, a sense of injustice, relief – and vice versa. There seems no way of accessing anything else; the case is closed. Which is why you seek corroboration, even if it turns out to be contradiction. But what if, even at a late stage, your emotions relating to those long-ago events and people change? That ugly letter of mine provoked remorse in me. Veronica's account of her parents' deaths – yes, even her father's – had touched me more than I would have thought possible. I felt a new sympathy for them – and her. Then, not long afterwards, I began remembering forgotten things. I don't know if there's a scientific explanation for this – to do with new affective states reopening blocked-off neural pathways. All I can say is that it happened, and that it astonished me.

So, anyway – and regardless of the barrister in my head – I emailed Veronica and suggested meeting again. Apologised for having done so much of the talking. Wanted to hear more about her life and her family. Had to come up to London at some point in the next few weeks. Did she fancy the same time, the same place?

How did people in the old days bear it when letters took so long to arrive? I suppose three weeks waiting for the postman then must equate to three days waiting for an email. How long can three days feel? Long enough for a full sense of reward. Veronica hadn't even deleted my heading – 'Hello again?' – which now struck me as rather winsome. But she can't have taken offence, because she was giving me a rendezvous, a week hence, at five in the afternoon, at an unfamiliar Tube station in north London.

I found this thrilling. Who wouldn't? True, it hardly said, 'Bring overnight clothes and passport,' but you get to a time when life's variations seem pitifully limited. Again, my first instinct was to phone Margaret; then I thought better of it. Anyway, Margaret doesn't like surprises. She was – is – someone who likes to plan things. Before we had Susie she used to monitor her fertility cycle and suggest when it might be most propitious to make love. Which either set me in a state of hot anticipation, or – conversely, indeed usually – had the opposite effect. Margaret would never give you a mysterious rendezvous up a distant Underground line. Rather, she would meet you beneath the station clock at Paddington for a specific purpose. Not that this wasn't how I wanted to live my life at the time, you must understand.

I spent a week trying to liberate new memories of Veronica, but nothing emerged. Maybe I was trying too hard, pressing on my brain. So instead I replayed what I had, the long-familiar images and the recent arrivals. I held them up to the light, turning them in my fingers, trying to see if they now meant something different. I began re-examining my younger self, as far as it's possible to do so. Of course I'd been crass and naïve – we all are; but I knew not to exaggerate these characteristics, because that's just a way of praising yourself for what you have become. I tried to be objective. The version of my relationship with Veronica, the one that I'd carried down the years, was the one I'd needed at the time. The young heart betrayed, the young body toyed with, the young social being condescended to. What had Old Joe Hunt answered when I knowingly claimed that history was the lies of the victors? 'As long as you remember that it is also the self-delusions of the defeated.' Do we remember that enough when it comes to our private lives?

The time-deniers say: forty's nothing, at fifty you're in your prime, sixty's the new forty, and so on. I know this much: that there is objective time, but also subjective time, the kind you wear on the inside of your wrist, next to where the pulse lies. And this personal time, which is the true time, is measured in your relationship to memory. So when this strange thing happened – when these new memories suddenly came upon me – it was as if, for that moment, time had been placed in reverse. As if, for that moment, the river ran upstream.

Of course, I was far too early, so I got off the train one stop before and sat on a bench reading a free newspaper. Or at least, staring at it. Then I took a train to the next station, where an escalator delivered me to a ticket hall in a part of London unknown to me. As I came through the barrier I saw a particular shape and way of standing. Immediately, she turned and walked off. I followed her past a bus stop into a side street where she unlocked a car. I got into the passenger seat and looked across. She was already starting the engine.

'That's funny. I've got a Polo too.'

She didn't reply. I shouldn't have been surprised. From my knowledge and memory of her, outdated though it was, car-talk was never going to be Veronica's thing. It wasn't mine either – though I knew better than to explain that.

It was a hot afternoon still. I opened my window. She glanced beyond me, frowning. I closed the window. Oh well, I said to myself.

'I was thinking the other day about when we watched the Severn Bore.'

She didn't reply.

'Do you remember that?' She shook her head. 'Really not? There was a gang of us, up at Minsterworth. There was a moon –'

'Driving,' she said.

'Fine.' If that was how she wanted it. After all, it was her expedition. I looked out of the window instead. Convenience stores, cheap restaurants, a betting shop, people queuing at a cash machine, women with bits of flesh spurting from between the joins of their clothes, a slew of litter, a shouting lunatic, an obese mother with three obese children, faces from all races: an all-purpose high street, normal London.

After a few minutes, we got to a posher bit: detached houses, front gardens, a hill. Veronica turned off and parked. I thought: OK, it's your game – I'll wait for the rules, whatever they might be. But part of me also thought: Fuck it, I'm not going to stop being myself just because you're back in your Wobbly Bridge state of mind.

'How's Brother Jack?' I asked cheerily. She could hardly answer 'Driving' to that question.

'Jack's Jack,' she replied, not looking at me.

Well, *that's* philosophically self-evident, as we used to say, back in the days of Adrian.

'Do you remember –'

'Waiting,' she interrupted.

Very well, I thought. First meeting, then driving, now waiting. What comes next? Shopping, cooking, eating and drinking, snogging, wanking and fucking? I very much doubt it. But as we sat side by side, a bald man and a whiskery woman, I realised what I should have spotted at once. Of the two of us, Veronica was much the more nervous. And whereas I was nervous about her, she clearly wasn't nervous about me. I was like some minor, necessary irritant. But why was I necessary?

I sat and waited. I rather wished I hadn't left that free newspaper on the train. I wondered why I hadn't driven here myself. Probably because I didn't know what the parking restrictions would be like. I wanted a drink of water. I also wanted to pee. I lowered the window. This time, Veronica didn't object.

'Look.'

I looked. A small group of people were coming along the pavement towards my side of the car. I counted five of them. In front was a man who, despite the heat, was wearing layers of heavy tweed, including a waistcoat and a kind of deerstalker helmet. His jacket and hat were covered with metal badges, thirty or forty of them at a guess, some glinting in the sun; there was a watch-chain slung between his waistcoat pockets. His expression was jolly: he looked like someone with an obscure function at a circus or fairground. Behind him came two men: the first had a black moustache and a kind of rolling gait; the second was small and malformed, with one shoulder much higher than the other – he paused to spit briefly into a front garden. And behind them was a tall, goofy fellow with glasses, holding the hand of a plump, Indianish woman.

'Pub,' said the man with the moustache as they drew level.

'No, not pub,' replied the man with the badges.

'Pub,' the first man insisted.

'Shop,' said the woman.

They all spoke in very loud voices, like children just let out of school.

'Shop,' repeated the lopsided man, with a gentle gob into a hedge.

I was looking as carefully as I could, because that was what I had been instructed to do. They must all, I suppose, have been between thirty and fifty, yet at the same time had a kind of fixed, ageless quality. Also, an obvious timidity, which was emphasised by the way the couple at the back were holding hands. It didn't look like amorousness, more defence against the world. They passed a few feet away, without glancing at the car. A few yards behind came a young man in shorts and an open-neck shirt; I couldn't tell if he was their shepherd, or had nothing to do with them.

There was a long silence. Clearly, I was going to have to do all the work.

'So?'

She didn't reply. Too general a question perhaps.

'What's wrong with them?'

'What's wrong with *you*?'

That didn't seem a relevant reply, for all its acrimonious tone. So I pressed on.

'Was that young chap with them?'

Silence.

'Are they care-in-the-community or something?'

My head banged back against the neck-rest as Veronica suddenly let out the clutch. She raced us round a block or two, charging the car at speed bumps as if it were a show-jumper. Her gear-changing, or the absence of it, was terrible. This lasted about four minutes, then she swerved into a parking space, riding up on the kerb with her front nearside wheel before bouncing back down again.

I found myself thinking: Margaret was always a nice driver. Not just safe, but one who treated a car properly. Back whenever it was I had driving lessons, my instructor had explained that when you change gear, your handling of clutch and gear lever should be so gentle and imperceptible that your passenger's head doesn't move a centimetre on its spinal column. I was very struck by that, and often noticed it when others drove me. If I lived with Veronica, I'd be down the chiropractor's most weeks.

'You just don't get it, do you? You never did, and you never will.'

'I'm not exactly being given much help.'

Then I saw them – whoever they were – coming towards me. That had been the point of the manoeuvre: to get ahead of them again. We were alongside a shop and a launderette, with a pub on the other side of the street. The man with the badges – 'barker', that was the word I'd been looking for, the cheery fellow at the entrance to a fairground booth who encourages you to step inside and view the bearded lady or two-headed panda – he was still leading. The other four were now surrounding the young man in shorts, so he was presumably with them. Some kind of care worker. Now I heard him say,

'No, Ken, no pub today. Friday's pub night.'

'Friday,' the man with the moustache repeated.

I was aware that Veronica had taken off her seat belt and was opening her door. As I started to do the same, she said,

'Stay.' I might have been a dog.

The pub-versus-shop debate was still going on when one of them noticed Veronica. The tweedy man took off his hat and held it against his heart, then bowed from the neck. The lopsided fellow started jumping up and down on the spot. The gangly chap let go of the woman's grasp. The care worker smiled and held out his hand to Veronica. In a moment she was surrounded by a benign ambush. The Indian woman was now holding Veronica's hand, and the man who wanted the pub was resting his head on her shoulder. She didn't seem to mind this attention at all. I watched her smile for the first time that afternoon. I tried to hear what was being said, but there were too many voices overlapping. Then I saw Veronica turn, and heard her say,

'Soon.'

'Soon,' two or three of them repeated.

The lopsided chap jumped some more on the spot, the gangly one gave a big goofy grin and shouted, 'Bye, Mary!' They began following her to the car, then noticed me in the passenger seat and stopped at once. Four of them started waving frantically goodbye, while the tweedy man boldly approached my side of the car. His hat was still clutched over his heart. He extended his other hand through the car window, and I shook it.

'We are going to the shop,' he told me formally.

'What are you going to buy?' I asked with equal solemnity.

This took him aback, and he thought about it for a while.

'Stuff we need,' he eventually replied. He nodded to himself and added, helpfully, 'Requisites.'

Then he did his formal little neck-bow, turned, and put his badge-heavy hat back on his head.

'He seems a very nice fellow,' I commented.

But she was putting the car into gear with one hand and waving with the other. I noticed that she was sweating. Yes, it was a hot day, but even so.

'They were all very pleased to see you.'

I could tell she wasn't going to reply to anything I said. Also that she was furious – certainly with me, but with herself as well. I can't say I felt I had done anything wrong. I was about to open my mouth when I saw she was aiming the car at a speed bump, not slowing at all, and it crossed my mind that I might bite the end of my tongue off with the impact. So I waited till we had safely hurdled the bump and said,

'I wonder how many badges that chap's got.'

Silence. Speed bump.

'Do they all live in the same house?'

Silence. Speed bump.

'So pub night is Friday.'

Silence. Speed bump.

'Yes, we did go to Minsterworth together. There was a moon that night.'

Silence. Speed bump. Now we turned into the high street, with nothing but flat tarmac between us and the station, as far as I remembered.

'This is a very interesting part of town.' I thought irritating her might do the trick — whatever the trick might be. Treating her like an insurance company lay well in the past.

'Yes, you're right, I should be getting back soon.'

'Still, it was nice catching up with you the other day over lunch.'

'Are there any Stefan Zweig titles you would particularly recommend?'

'There are a lot of fat people around nowadays. Obese. That's one of the changes since we were young, isn't it? I can't remember anyone at Bristol being obese.'

'Why did that goofy chap call you Mary?'

At least I had my seat belt on. This time Veronica's parking technique consisted of getting both nearside wheels up on the kerb at a speed of about twenty miles an hour, then stamping on the brakes.

'Out,' she said, staring ahead.

I nodded, undid my seat belt, and slowly got out of the car. I held the door open longer than necessary, just to annoy her one last time, and said,

'You'll ruin your tyres if you go on like that.'

The door was wrenched from my hand as she drove off.

I sat on the train home not thinking at all, really, just feeling. And not even thinking about what I was feeling. Only that evening did I begin to address what had happened.

The main reason I felt foolish and humiliated was because of – what had I called it to myself, only a few days previously? – 'the eternal hopefulness of the human heart'. And before that, 'the attraction of overcoming someone's contempt'. I don't think I normally suffer from vanity, but I'd clearly been more afflicted than I realised. What had begun as a determination to obtain property bequeathed to me had morphed into something much larger, something which bore on the whole of my life, on time and memory. And desire. I thought – at some level of my being, I actually thought – that I could go back to the beginning and change things. That I could make the blood flow backwards. I had the vanity to imagine – even if I didn't put it more strongly than this – that I could make Veronica like me again, and that it was important to do so. When she had emailed about 'closing the circle', I had completely failed to pick the tone as one of sardonic mockery, and taken it as an invitation, almost a come-on.

Her attitude towards me, now that I looked at it, had been consistent – not just in recent months, but over however many years. She had found me wanting, had preferred Adrian, and always considered these judgements correct. This was, I now realised, self-evident in every way, philosophical or other. But, without understanding my own motives, I had wanted to prove to her, even at this late stage, that she had got me wrong. Or rather, that her initial view of me – when we were learning one another's hearts and bodies, when she approved of some of my books and records, when she liked me enough to take me home – had been correct. I thought I could overcome contempt and turn remorse back into guilt, then be forgiven. I had been tempted, somehow, by the notion that we could excise most of our separate existences, could cut and splice the magnetic tape on which our lives are recorded, go back to that fork in the path and take the road less travelled, or rather not travelled at all. Instead, I had just left common sense behind. Old fool, I said to myself. And there's no fool like an old fool: that's what my long-dead mother used to mutter when reading stories in the papers about older men falling for younger women, and throwing up their marriages for a simpering smile, hair that came out of a bottle, and a taut pair of tits. Not that she would have put it like that. And I couldn't even offer the excuse of cliché, that I was just doing what other men of my age banally did. No, I was an odder old fool, grafting pathetic hopes of affection on to the least likely recipient in the world.

That next week was one of the loneliest of my life. There seemed nothing left to look forward to. I was alone with two voices speaking clearly in my head: Margaret's saying, 'Tony, you're on your own now,' and Veronica's saying, 'You just don't get it . . . You never did, and you never will.' And knowing that Margaret wouldn't crow if I rang up – knowing that she would happily agree to another of our little lunches, and we could go on exactly as before – made me feel all the lonelier. Who was it said that the longer we live, the less we understand?

Still, as I tend to repeat, I have some instinct for survival, for self-preservation. And believing you have such an instinct is almost as good as actually having it, because it means you act in the same way. So after a while, I rallied. I knew I must go back to how I had been before this silly, senile fantasy took hold of me. I must attend to my affairs, what-ever they might be, apart from tidying up my flat and running the library at the local hospital. Oh yes, and I could concentrate again on getting back my stuff.

'Dear Jack,' I wrote. 'Wonder if you could give me a spot more help with Veronica. Afraid I'm finding her just as mystifying as in the old days. Well, do we ever learn? Anyway, the ice flow hasn't melted with regard to my old pal's diary that your mother left me in her will. Any further advice about that? Also, another slight puzzle. I had quite a jolly lunch with V in town the other week. Then she asked me up the Northern line one afternoon. It seems she wanted to show me some care-in-the-community folk, then got cross when she'd done so. Can you shed any light on this one? Trust all's fine with you. Regards, Tony W.'

I hoped the bonhomie didn't ring as false to him as it did to me. Then I wrote to Mr Gunnell, asking him to act for me in the matter of Mrs Ford's will. I told him – in confidence – that my recent dealings with the legator's daughter had suggested a certain instability, and I now thought it best that a fellow professional write to Mrs Marriott and request a speedy resolution of the issue.

I allowed myself a private nostalgic farewell. I thought of Veronica dancing, hair all over her face. I thought of her announcing to her family, 'I'm going to walk Tony to his room,' whispering to me that I was to sleep the sleep of the wicked, and my promptly wanking into the little basin before she was even downstairs again. I thought of my inner wrist looking shiny, of my shirt sleeve furled to the elbow.

Mr Gunnell wrote to say that he would do as I instructed. Brother Jack never replied.

★

I'd noticed – well, I would – that parking restrictions only applied between the hours of ten and midday. Probably to discourage commuters from driving this far into town, dumping their cars for the day, and carrying on in by Tube. So I decided to take my car this time: a VW Polo whose tyres would last a lot longer than Veronica's. After a purgatorial hour or so on the North Circular, I found myself in position, parked where we had been before, facing up the slight incline of a suburban street, with the late-afternoon sun catching the dust on a privet hedge. Bands of schoolchildren were on their way home, boys with shirts out of their trousers, girls with provocatively high skirts; many on mobile phones, some eating, a few smoking. When I'd been at school we were told that as long as you were in the uniform you had to behave in a way that reflected well on the institution. So no eating or drinking in the street; while anyone caught smoking would be beaten. Nor was fraternisation with the opposite sex allowed: the girls' school linked to ours and quartered nearby used to let its pupils out fifteen minutes before the boys were freed, giving them time to get well clear of their predatory and priapic male counterparts. I sat there remembering all this, registering the differences, without coming to any conclusions. I neither applauded nor disapproved. I was indifferent; I had suspended my right to thoughts and judgements. All I cared about was why I had been brought to this street a couple of weeks previously. So I sat with my window down and waited.

After two hours or so, I gave up. I came back the next day, and the next, without success. Then I drove to the street with the pub and the shop, and parked outside. I waited, went into the shop and bought a few things, waited some more, drove home. I had absolutely no sense of wasting my time: rather, it was the opposite way round – that this was what my time was now for. And in any case the shop turned out to be pretty useful. It was one of those places which spans the range from delicatessen to hardware store. Over this period I bought vegetables and dishwasher powder, sliced meats and loo paper; I used the cash machine and stocked up on booze. After the first few days they started calling me 'mate'.

I thought at one point of contacting the borough's social-services department and asking if they had a care-in-the-community home which sheltered a man all covered in badges; but doubted this would get me anywhere. I would baulk at their first question: why do you want to know? I didn't know why I wanted to know. But as I say, I had no sense of urgency. It was like not pressing on the brain to summon a memory. If I didn't press on – what? – time, then something, perhaps even a solution, might come to the surface.

And in due course I remembered words I'd overheard. 'No, Ken, no pub today. Friday night's pub night.' So the following Friday I drove over and sat with a newspaper in the William IV. It was one of those pubs gentrified by economic pressure. There was a food menu with char-grilled this and that, a telly quietly emitting the BBC News Channel, and blackboards everywhere: one advertising the weekly quiz night, another the monthly book club, a third the upcoming TV sports fixtures, while a fourth bore an epigrammatic thought for the day, no doubt transcribed from some corporate book of wit and wisdom. I slowly drank halves while doing the crossword, but nobody came.

The second Friday, I thought: I may as well have my supper here, so ordered chargrilled hake with handcut chips and a large glass of Chilean Sauvignon Blanc. It wasn't bad at all. Then, on the third Friday, just as I was forking my penne with gorgonzola and walnut sauce, in walked the lopsided man and the chap with the moustache. They took their seats familiarly at a table, whereupon the barman, clearly used to their requirements, brought each of them a half of bitter, which they proceeded to sip meditatively. They didn't look around, let alone seek to make eye contact; and in return, no one took any notice of them. After about twenty minutes a motherly black woman came in, went up to the bar, paid, and gently escorted the two men away. I merely observed and waited. Time was on my side, yes it was. Songs do occasionally tell the truth.

I now became a regular at the pub as well as the shop. I didn't join the book club or participate in quiz night, but regularly sat at a small table by the window and worked my way through the menu. What was I hoping for? Probably to get into conversation at some point with the young care worker I'd seen escorting the quintet that first afternoon; or even, perhaps, with the badge man, who seemed the most affable and approachable. I was patient without any sense of being so; I no longer counted the hours; and then, one early evening, I saw all five of them approaching, shepherded by the same woman. Somehow, I wasn't even surprised. The two regulars came into the pub; the other three went into the shop with the minder.

I got up, leaving my biro and newspaper on the table as signs that I would return. At the shop's entrance I picked up a yellow plastic basket and wandered slowly round. At the end of an aisle the three of them were clustered in front of a choice of washing-up liquids, gravely debating which to buy. The space was narrow, and I said a loud 'Excuse me' as I approached. The gangly fellow with glasses immediately pressed himself, face inwards, against shelves of kitchen stuff, and all three fell silent. As I passed, the badge man looked me in the face. 'Evening,' I said with a smile. He carried on looking, then bowed from the neck. I left it at that and returned to the pub.

A few minutes later the three of them joined the two drinkers. The care woman went to the bar and ordered. I was struck by the fact that while they'd been boisterous and childlike in the street, they were shy and whispering in the shop and pub. Soft drinks were carried across to the newcomers. I thought I heard the word 'birthday' but might have been mistaken. I decided that it was time to order food. My path to the bar would take me close by them. I had no actual plan. The three who had come in from the shop were still standing, and they turned slightly as I approached. I addressed a second cheery 'Evening!' to the badge man, who responded as before. The gangly bloke was now in front of me and as I was about to make my way past I stopped and looked at him properly. He was about forty, just over six feet, with a pallid skin and thick-lensed glasses. I could sense he was keen to turn his back again. But instead, he did something unexpected. He took off his glasses and looked me full in the face. His eyes were brown and gentle.

Almost without thinking, I said to him quietly, 'I'm a friend of Mary's.'

I watched as he first began to smile, then panic. He turned away, gave a muted whine, shuffled close to the Indian woman, and took her hand. I carried on to the bar, put half a buttock on a stool and started examining the menu. A moment or two later, I became aware of the black carer beside me.

'I'm sorry,' I said. 'I hope I didn't do anything wrong.'

'I'm not sure,' she replied. 'It's not good to startle him. Especially now.'

'I met him once before, with Mary when she came over one afternoon. I'm a friend of hers.'

She looked at me, as if trying to assess my motives and my truthfulness. 'Then you'll understand,' she said quietly, 'won't you?'

'Yes, I do.'

And the thing was, I did. I didn't need to talk to the badge man or the male carer. Now I knew.

I saw it in his face. It's not often that's true, is it? At least, not for me. We listen to what people say, we read what they write – that's our evidence, that's our corroboration. But if the face contradicts the speaker's words, we interrogate the face. A shifty look in the eye, a rising blush, the uncontrollable twitch of a face muscle – and then we know. We recognise the hypocrisy or the false claim, and the truth stands evident before us.

But this was different, simpler. There was no contradiction – I simply saw it in his face. In the eyes, their colour and expression, and in the cheeks, their pallor and underlying structure. Corroboration came from his height, and the way his bones and muscles arranged that height. This was Adrian's son. I didn't need a birth certificate or DNA test – I saw it and felt it. And of course the dates matched: he would be about this age now.

My first reaction was, I admit, solipsistic. I couldn't avoid remembering what I'd written in the part of my letter addressed to Veronica: 'It's just a question of whether you can get pregnant before he discovers you're a bore.' I hadn't even meant it at the time – I was just flailing around, trying to find a way to hurt. In fact, all the time I was going out with Veronica, I found her many things – alluring, mysterious, disapproving – but never boring. And even in my recent dealings with her, though the adjectives might be updated – exasperating, stubborn, haughty, yet still, in a way, alluring – I never found her boring. So it was as false as it was hurtful.

But that was only the half of it. When I'd been trying to damage them, I'd written: 'Part of me hopes you have a child, because I'm a great believer in time's revenge. But revenge must be on the right people, i.e. you two.' And then: 'So I don't wish you that. It would be unjust to inflict on some innocent foetus the prospect of discovering that it was the fruit of your loins, if you'll excuse the poeticism.' Remorse, etymologically, is the action of biting again: that's what the feeling does to you. Imagine the strength of the bite when I reread my words. They seemed like some ancient curse I had forgotten even uttering. Of course I don't – I didn't – believe in curses. That's to say, in words producing events. But the very action of naming something that subsequently happens – of wishing specific evil, and that evil coming to pass – this still has a shiver of the other-worldly about it. The fact that the young me who cursed and the old me who witnessed the curse's outcome had quite different feelings – this was monstrously irrelevant. If, just before all this started, you had told me that Adrian, instead of killing himself, had counterfactually married

Veronica, that they had had a child together, then perhaps others, and then grandchildren, I would have answered: That's fine, each to their own life; you went your way and I went mine, no hard feelings. And now these idle clichés ran up against the unshiftable truth of what had happened. Time's revenge on the innocent foetus. I thought of that poor, damaged man turning away from me in the shop and pressing his face into rolls of kitchen towel and jumbo packs of quilted toilet tissue so as to avoid my presence. Well, his instinct had been a true one: I was a man against whom backs should be turned. If life did reward merit, then I deserved shunning.

Only a few days previously I'd been entertaining a dim fantasy about Veronica, all the while admitting that I knew nothing of her life in the forty and more years since I'd last seen her. Now I had some answers to the questions I hadn't asked. She had become pregnant by Adrian, and – who knows? – perhaps the trauma of his suicide had affected the child in her womb. She had given birth to a son who had at some stage been diagnosed as . . . what? As not being able to function independently in society; as needing constant support, emotional and financial. I wondered when that diagnosis had been made. Was it soon after birth, or had there been a lulling pause of a few years, during which Veronica could take comfort in what had been saved from the wreckage? But afterwards – how long had she sacrificed her life for him, perhaps taking some crappy part-time job while he was at a special-needs school? And then, presumably, he had got bigger and harder to manage, and eventually the terrible struggle became too much, and she allowed him to be taken into care. Imagine what that must have felt like; imagine the loss, the sense of failure, the guilt. And here was

I, complaining to myself when my daughter occasionally forgot to send me an email. I also remembered the ungrateful thoughts I'd had since first meeting Veronica again on the Wobbly Bridge. I thought she looked a bit shabby and unkempt; I thought she was difficult, unfriendly, charmless. In fact, I was lucky she gave me the time of day. And I'd expected her to hand over Adrian's diary? In her place, I'd probably have burnt it too, as I now believed she had done.

There was no one I could tell this to – not for a long while. As Margaret said, I was on my own – and so I should be. Not least because I had a swathe of my past to re-evaluate, with nothing but remorse for company. And after rethinking Veronica's life and character, I would have to go back into my past and deal with Adrian. My philosopher friend, who gazed on life and decided that any responsible, thinking individual should have the right to reject this gift that had never been asked for – and whose noble gesture re-emphasised with each passing decade the compromise and littleness that most lives consist of. 'Most lives': my life.

So this image of him – this living, dead rebuke to me and the rest of my existence – was now overturned. 'First-class degree, first-class suicide,' Alex and I had agreed. What sort of Adrian did I have instead? One who had got his girlfriend pregnant, been unable to face the consequences, and had 'taken the easy way out', as they used to put it. Not that there can be anything easy about it, this final assertion of individuality against the great generality that oppresses it. But now I had to recalibrate Adrian, change him from a Camus-quoting repudiator for whom suicide was the only true philosophical question, into . . . what? No more than a version of Robson, who 'wasn't exactly Eros-and-Thanatos material', as Alex had put it, when that hitherto unremarkable member of the Science Sixth had left this world with a parting 'Sorry, Mum'.

At the time, the four of us had speculated on what Robson's girl must have been like – from prim virgin to clap-riddled whore. None of us had thought about the child, or the future. Now, for the first time, I wondered what had happened to Robson's girl, and to their child. The mother would be about my age, and quite probably still alive, while the child would be nearing fifty. Did it still believe that 'Dad' had died in an accident? Perhaps it had been sent for adoption, and grew up thinking itself unwanted. But nowadays adoptees have the right to trace their birth mothers. I imagined this happening, and the awkward, poignant reunion it might have led to. I found myself wanting, even at this distance, to apologise to Robson's girl for the idle way we had discussed her, without reckoning her pain and shame. Part of me wanted to get in touch and ask her to excuse our faults of long ago – even though she had been quite unaware of them at the time.

But thinking about Robson, and Robson's girl, was just a way of avoiding what was now the truth about Adrian. Robson had been fifteen, sixteen? Still living at home, with parents who no doubt weren't exactly liberals. And if his girl had been under sixteen, there might have been a rape charge too. So there was really no comparison. Adrian had grown up, had left home, and was far more intelligent than poor Robson. Besides, back then, if you got a girl pregnant, and if she didn't want to have an abortion, you married her: those were the rules. Yet Adrian couldn't even face this conventional solution. 'Do you think it was because he was too clever?' my mother had irritatingly asked. No, nothing to do with cleverness; and even less with moral courage. He didn't grandly refuse an existential gift; he was afraid of the pram in the hall.

What did I know of life, I who had lived so carefully? Who had neither won nor lost, but just let life happen to him? Who had the usual ambitions and settled all too quickly for them not being realised? Who avoided being hurt and called it a capacity for survival? Who paid his bills, stayed on good terms with everyone as far as possible, for whom ecstasy and despair soon became just words once read in novels? One whose self-rebukes never really inflicted pain? Well, there was all this to reflect upon, while I endured a special kind of remorse: a hurt inflicted at long last on one who always thought he knew how to avoid being hurt – and inflicted for precisely that reason.

'Out!' Veronica had instructed, having mounted the kerb at twenty miles an hour. Now I gave the word its wider resonance: Out of my life, I never wanted you near it again in the first place. I should never have agreed to meet, let alone have lunch, let alone take you to see my son. Out, out!

If I'd had an address for her, I would have sent a proper letter. I headed my email 'Apology', then changed it to 'APOLOGY', but that looked too screamy, so I changed it back again. I could only be straightforward.

Dear Veronica,

I realise that I am probably the last person you want to hear from, but I hope you will read this message through to the end. I don't expect you to reply to it. But I have spent some time re-evaluating things, and would like to apologise to you. I don't expect you to think better of me – but then, you could hardly think any worse. That letter of mine was unforgiveable. All I can say is that my vile words were the expression of a moment. They were a genuine shock for me to read again after all these years.

I don't expect you to hand over Adrian's diary. If you've burnt it, there's an end to it. If you haven't, then obviously, as it was written by the father of your son, it belongs to you. I'm puzzled why your mother left it to me in the first place, but that's no matter.

I'm sorry to have been so vexatious. You were trying to show me something and I was too crass to understand. I would like to wish you and your son a peaceful life, as far as that's possible in the circumstances. And if at any time I can do anything for either of you, I hope you won't hesitate to get in touch.

Yours, Tony

It was the best I could do. It wasn't as good as I'd wanted, but at least I meant every word of it. I had no hidden agenda. I didn't secretly hope for anything out of it. Not a diary, not Veronica's good opinion, not even an acceptance of my apology.

I can't say whether I felt better or worse after sending it. I felt not very much. Exhausted, emptied-out. I had no desire to tell Margaret about what had happened. I thought more often of Susie, and of the luck any parent has when a child is born with four limbs, a normal brain, and the emotional make-up that allows the child, the girl, the woman to lead any sort of life. May you be ordinary, as the poet once wished the new-born baby.

My life continued. I recommended books to the sick, the recovering, the dying. I read a book or two myself. I put out my recycling. I wrote to Mr Gunnell and asked him not to pursue the matter of the diary. One late afternoon, on a whim, I drove round the North Circular, did some shopping and had supper at the William IV. I was asked if I'd been away on holiday. In the shop I said yes, in the pub I said no. The answers hardly seemed of consequence. Not much did. I thought of the things that had happened to me over the years, and of how little I had made happen.

At first I assumed it was an old email, mistakenly re-sent. But my heading had been left there: 'Apology'. Below, my message was undeleted. Her reply went: 'You still don't get it. You never did, and you never will. So stop even trying.'

I left the exchange in my inbox and occasionally reread it. If I hadn't decided on cremation and a scattering, I could have used the phrase as an epitaph on a chunk of stone or marble: 'Tony Webster – He Never Got It'. But that would be too melodramatic, even self-pitying. How about 'He's On His Own Now'? That would be better, truer. Or maybe I'll stick with: 'Every Day is Sunday'.

Occasionally, I would drive over to the shop and the pub again. They were places where I always felt a sense of calm, odd as that may sound; also, a sense of purpose, perhaps the last proper purpose of my life. As before, I never thought I was wasting my time. This was what my time might as well be for. And both were friendly places – at least, friendlier than their equivalents where I lived. I had no plan: so what else is new? I hadn't had a 'plan' for years. And my revival of feeling – if that's what it had been – towards Veronica could scarcely be counted as a plan. More of a brief, morbid impulse, an appendix to a short history of humiliation.

One day, I said to the barman, 'Do you think you could do me thin chips for a change?'

'How do you mean?'

'You know, like in France – the thin ones.'

'No, we don't do them.'

'But it says on the menu your chips are hand-cut.'

'Yes.'

'Well, can't you cut them thinner?'

The barman's normal affableness took a pause. He looked at me as if he wasn't sure whether I was a pedant or an idiot, or quite possibly both.

'Hand-cut chips means fat chips.'

'But if you handcut chips, couldn't you cut them thinner?'

'We don't cut them. That's how they arrive.'

'You don't cut them on the premises?'

'That's what I said.'

'So what you call "hand-cut chips" are actually cut elsewhere, and quite probably by a machine?'

'Are you from the council or something?'

'Not in the least. I'm just puzzled. I never realised that

"hand–cut" meant "fat" rather than "necessarily cut by hand".'

'Well, you do now.'

'I'm sorry. I just didn't get it.'

I retired to my table and waited for my supper.

And then, just like that, the five of them came in, accompanied by the young minder I'd seen from Veronica's car. The badge man stopped as he passed my table, and gave me his bow from the neck; a couple of the badges on his deerstalker chinked quietly together. The others followed. When Adrian's son saw me, he turned his shoulder as if to keep me – and bad luck – away. The five of them crossed to the far wall but didn't sit down. The care worker went to the bar and ordered drinks.

My hake and hand-cut chips arrived, the latter served in a metal pot lined with newspaper. Perhaps I had been smiling to myself when the young man arrived at my table.

'Do you mind if I have a word?'

'Not at all.'

I gestured to the chair opposite. As he sat down I noticed, over his shoulder, the five of them looking across at me, holding on to their glasses, not drinking.

'I'm Terry.'

'Tony.'

We shook hands in that awkward, elbow-high way that being seated imposes. He was silent at first.

'Chip?' I suggested.

'No thanks.'

'Did you know that when they put "hand-cut" chips on a menu, it just means "fat", it doesn't mean they're actually cut by hand?'

He looked at me rather as the barman had.

'It's about Adrian.'

'Adrian,' I repeated. Why had I never wondered about his name? And what else could he have possibly been called?

'Your presence upsets him.'

'I'm sorry,' I replied. 'The last thing I want to do is upset him. I don't want to upset anyone any more. *Ever.*' He looked at me as if he suspected irony. 'It's all right. He won't see me again. I'll finish my food and be off, and none of you will ever see me again.'

He nodded. 'Do you mind me asking who you are?'

Who I am? 'Of course not. My name's Tony Webster. Many years ago I was a friend of Adrian's father. I was at school with him. I used to know Adrian's mother – Veronica – too. Quite well. Then we lost touch. But we've seen quite a bit of one another over the last weeks. No, months, I should say.'

'Weeks and months?'

'Yes,' I said. 'Though I shan't be seeing Veronica again either. She doesn't want to know me any more.' I tried to make it sound factual rather than pathetic.

He looked at me. 'You understand that we can't discuss our clients' histories. It's a matter of confidentiality.'

'Of course.'

'But what you've just said doesn't make any sense.'

I thought about this. 'Oh – Veronica – yes, I'm sorry. I remember he – Adrian – called her Mary. I suppose that's what she calls herself with him. It's her second name. But I knew her – know her – as Veronica.'

Over his shoulder I could see the five of them standing anxiously, still not drinking, watching us. I felt ashamed that my presence bothered them.

'If you were a friend of his father's –'

'And his mother's.'

'Then I think you don't understand.' At least he put it differently from others.

'I don't?'

'Mary isn't his mother. Mary's his sister. Adrian's mother died about six months ago. He took it very badly. That's why he's been . . . having problems lately.'

Automatically, I ate a chip. Then another. There wasn't enough salt on them. That's the disadvantage of fat chips. They have too much potatoey inside. With thin chips, not only is there more crispy outside, but the salt is better distributed too.

All I could do was offer Terry my hand and a repeat of my promise. 'And I hope he'll be all right. I'm sure you look after him very well. They all seem to get on, the five of them.'

He stood up. 'Well, we do our best, but we get hit by budget cuts almost every year.'

'Good luck to you all,' I said.

'Thanks.'

When I paid, I left twice the normal tip. At least that was one way of being useful.

And later, at home, going over it all, after some time, I understood. I got it. Why Mrs Ford had Adrian's diary in the first place. Why she had written: 'P.S. It may sound odd, but I think the last months of his life were happy.' What the second carer meant when she said, 'Especially now.' Even what Veronica meant by 'blood money'. And finally, what Adrian was talking about on the page I'd been permitted to see. 'Thus, how might you express an accumulation containing the integers b, a^1, a^2, s, v?' And then a couple of formulae expressing possible accumulations. It was obvious now. The first a was Adrian; and the other was me, Anthony – as he used to address me when he wanted to call me to seriousness. And b signified 'baby'. One born to a mother – 'The Mother' – at a dangerously late age. A child damaged as a result. Who was now a man of forty, lost in grief. And who called his sister Mary. I looked at the chain of responsibility. I saw my initial in there. I remembered that in my ugly letter I had urged Adrian to consult Veronica's mother. I replayed the words that would forever haunt me. As would Adrian's unfinished sentence. 'So, for instance, if Tony . . .' I knew I couldn't change, or mend, anything now.

You get towards the end of life – no, not life itself, but of something else: the end of any likelihood of change in that life. You are allowed a long moment of pause, time enough to ask the question: what else have I done wrong? I thought of a bunch of kids in Trafalgar Square. I thought of a young woman dancing, for once in her life. I thought of what I couldn't know or understand now, of all that couldn't ever be known or understood. I thought of Adrian's definition of history. I thought of his son cramming his face into a shelf of quilted toilet tissue in order to avoid me. I thought of a woman frying eggs in a carefree, slapdash way, untroubled when one of them broke in the pan; then the same woman, later, making a secret, horizontal gesture beneath a sunlit wisteria. And I thought of a cresting wave of water, lit by a moon, rushing past and vanishing upstream, pursued by a band of yelping students whose torchbeams criss-crossed in the dark.

There is accumulation. There is responsibility. And beyond these, there is unrest. There is great unrest.

Also available from Vintage

JULIAN BARNES

Flaubert's Parrot

Shortlisted for the Booker Prize

Flaubert's Parrot deals with Flaubert, parrots, bears and railways; with our sense of the past and our sense of abroad; with France and England, life and art, sex and death, George Sand and Louise Colet, aesthetics and redcurrant jam; and with its enigmatic narrator, a retired English doctor, whose life and secrets are slowly revealed.

A compelling weave of fiction and imaginatively ordered fact, *Flaubert's Parrot* is by turns moving and entertaining, witty and scholarly, and a tour de force of seductive originality.

'Unputdownable... A mesmeric original'
Philip Larkin

'An intricate and delightful novel'
Graham Greene

'Delightful and enriching... A book to revel in'
Joseph Heller

VINTAGE

JULIAN BARNES

The Noise of Time

The *Sunday Times* Number One Bestseller

In May 1937 a man in his early thirties waits by the lift of a Leningrad apartment block. He waits all through the night, expecting to be taken away to the Big House. Any celebrity he has known in the previous decade is no use to him now. And few who are taken to the Big House ever return.

This is a story about the collision of Art and Power, about human compromise, human cowardice and human courage, it is the work of a true master.

'Barnes's masterpiece... Exquisite'
Observer

'Gleaming with intelligence and literary flair'
Sunday Times

'Moving, tense and darkly comical'
Daily Telegraph

VINTAGE